Willesden

New Short S

www.newshortstories.com

Published in the United States and the United Kingdom in 2017
by Pretend Genius Press

ISBN 978-0-9995277-2-6

Willesden Herald

New Short Stories 10

www.NewShortStories.com

Contents

Introduction

It's probably the second or third time that Stephen
Moran asks if I'd like to judge the Willesden Prize, that
I accept. The first time was some years back when the
prize was still a toddler. It's now in double digits. This
is the tenth book in the New Short Stories series, while
the prize has been around a little over a decade, having
had a gap year or two. The Willesden Prize is a non-
profit venture and it's a more or less annual labour of
love to the short story. I know this before I accept. I'm
pretty sure Stephen had tellings off from his partner
more than once over how much of his time it used to
take up. Now he's on book number ten, his process is
doubtless a bit more streamlined. He knows what to
expect and what to avoid, how to manage writer
expectations, all that. This year, the entry deadline fell
in late August, the sift took place in September, judging
in October, and the hope is the book will be at the
printers or perhaps even available for sale, before the
year is out.

　　With all entries made online, it isn't difficult to get
hold of the stories. An email from Stephen reaches me
on October 10th giving access to the 20 longlisted
stories. I offered to read more but this is the number
we go with. The selected stories have enticing titles and
make interesting reading. The tricky thing is to stick to
the decisions made. A few stories keep leaping out of
the amber pile, back into green. As a result, I'm not the
swiftest judge the prize has had: come Halloween while

trick or treaters knock on the door, I'm still dithering over my top three, wavering over the winner, asking for a gender count on my shortlist, to rule out any unconscious bias. (No change is needed, fortunately). Stephen Moran is patient and efficient on the other end of the phone, or in emails. In the end there are no more excuses — the clock is ticking and by midnight an overall winner must be found from the small cacophony of prize-worthy stories. At one point I concoct an ingenious ruse to include eleven stories in the book instead of ten. (If this sounds like a classic rookie error, let me add, it never came up in previous short fiction competitions that I judged.) When Stephen hears of this little scheme, he responds just as calmly as before, while firmly ruling it out. Something about fairness to the ten. It's not the extra page count. Money doesn't get a mention. He's not bothered about costs so long as break-even point is reached, which has happened this year. Other years, he's had the distraction of running a fundraiser in order to publish the book.

Moving on then, perhaps, to the stories. If you are the sort of person who reads introductions, this may be what you want. You may be seeking flowery sentences to compliment the authors, little summaries to help you write a quick review. Or you may be someone's proud mum or boyfriend or girlfriend, thinking, 'I hope X gets a mention', or 'This is worrying, I had a feeling perhaps it wasn't a proper book.' If you are, please don't worry. This is a real book. But wouldn't it take all the fun out of reading the stories if the introduction laboured over the range of characters and settings, if it revealed the unexpected? Some people cannot pick a chocolate from a box without referring to what's called the 'tasting notes', on a posh box of chocolates... Well, if literary tasting notes are what you want of an introduction, this one won't be much use. I could say more about the stories gathered here, but choose not to. If you enjoy short stories because they bring you to unexpected places in strange company, if you don't care for flattery or the art of the finely-honed blurb, you'll understand. Far better to send you on a journey to experience these stories for yourself. Better, also, to honour the tradition of previous years of the Willesden Prize by not singling out any particular winner. So congratulations to all ten authors whose work is gathered here on their prize-winning stories, and to you the reader on having found them. Read on, and enjoy.

Lane Ashfeldt,
from a rainstorm on the edge of Europe,
November 2017

Dark Song

Roberta Dewa

I slip into the water. I didn't plan to swim, but there's still static fizzing in my veins from last night's concert and as the river laps me up I'm cooling down, the static disappearing into a string of bubbles streaming out all around me and rising up from the deep channel, like there's a diver down there somewhere.

It's been a while since they said I looked like my father. Time was they'd come up to me every night after the set with their autograph books and shake their heads when I signed my name. They'd look at me and say I had his corkscrew hair, they'd listen to me and it's his voice they were hearing, his howling at the moon; his silver howls, clean as air. Then they got tired, or they got used to me, or maybe they just ran out of memory. But last night there was this one guy, shouting out between the numbers, Hey, junior. Do the dark song. Nah, I said, like I always do, and I spun right round so when I came back it was me he'd have to see.

The water's good, it puts the fire out. A world of it, washing from one side of the bay to the other, filling up the dirty muddy space between the banks. I swim out from the shallows and my feet dip down into it, tasting the darkness. And maybe there is life down there. Blind life, never singing up toward the light.

I nearly met him once, your father, the guy said.

Yeah, I said, me too. I nearly met him once.

The guy stared.

I cut out into the waves. They turn me this way and that so that one minute I'm looking back to the shore, the next out to the sandbank and the ocean beyond. Then I dip and surface again and there's the bank, but whether it's the place I started from or the one I'm swimming to

I don't know.

This is how it was, that one time I nearly met my father. Must have been seven or eight, I don't remember. We were okay without him until that call. He was music, and we were family; and my Mom had told me he could only do the music. But that birthday he'd sent me a kid's guitar and then there was a call to say he was coming to visit. We stayed home a while and he didn't come and then he called again and Mom said we were going out to the park and I took my guitar and I strummed my three notes and we waited. We waited by the lake, so we could see him from across the water as he came through the gates. I knew the shape of him, the size of him, I'd seen his picture in the music papers, stick-thin with the corkscrew hair. I'd heard him talk on the TV, I'd watched him singing with his eyes shut, always with his eyes shut. One time I asked my Mom if he was blind. No, she said, it's just the world hurts his eyes.

It's getting dark. There's a foghorn blaring close to my head and the white ridge of a wake knocks me sideways and I'm flapping in the water like a flounder. A wave makes toward me and for a minute I'm back under the sun on the West Coast but then it slaps against me, slow and thick and heavy. Harbor water, silting up my boots, filling up my clothes.

That day the park was busy but I watched the gate. And time just rolled by on the clock, one and two and three, and I strummed them all on my guitar and Mom went real quiet. And the sun was bright and I shut my eyes.

And when I opened them he was there, the other side of the lake, coat collar turned up, hands in the pockets of his cords, his guitar slung round him like he was going somewhere. I got up to run round to him but

Mom got hold of my hand.

No, she said, no. Let him come to you.

I looked across. It was too far to see if his eyes were open but I saw him put his hand up, as if he was going to wave, but he didn't move it. It was just up there in the air, flat palm towards us, like he was pushing on something I couldn't see.

Then he turned as if he was leaving and I pulled my hand away and said Mom, don't let him go; and I was splashing in the shallows of the lake with water in my sneakers trying to get to the other side and Mom coming after me, shouting, trying to pull me out.

And I looked across again but he was walking back towards the gate and all I could see was the shut face of his guitar.

It must have been about a year or so before he shot up one time too many. And when Mom came to my room to tell me I'd already turned my back.

But somehow he stuck around. Sometimes I'd see him in black and white on the TV on one of those old talk shows, scrunched up in a chair with his hair flaring out like static round his face. There'd be a suit behind a desk saying, What is it with you young people, and he'd answer soft as sugar something like, We just want freedom, man, we just want peace and love. But it was the voice leaking out of the amplifiers, the voice I didn't want to listen to but couldn't help, that was where I heard the colors. His voice running up and down the scales and then right off them, purple and charcoal when it was warm and low down; and then when he was screaming it was real sharp blue, like ice cracking. I'd try to switch off but those colors just kept going like a lightshow clean around my head, kept going even when I started in the clubs. And there'd always be a guy in the crowd like this guy, spotting them, asking for the old songs. A dead man's songs. Nah, I'd say, always, like last night. Always.

I gave in, in the end. I did the tributes, the old songs, the whole deal. I guess I wanted to go back to the park and tell him I get it now, the freedom thing, the hand keeping the world out of his eyes. I wanted to tell him I'm all grown up, I can sing your songs and walk away from them at the end of the night. Turn around and be myself again. And finally I was slipping in my own songs until I could see my colors, muddier than his maybe, letting them run and blend into his. Not the dark song, though. I guess I didn't have enough peace and love in me. I drew a line, and that was it.

The moon's up. Spiking the froth on the waves with light. The sandbank gleams wet and it's like there's music playing out there somewhere. The sound is dense, muddy, as if the music's coming through the water. My legs are stirring up the sand and mud and it's like the sea's thick with music. There's a voice singing, but I don't know whose it is. I can hear the words, though, and I know what words they are, I know what song this is. There's a boat coming towards me, growling over the surface of the water, but I can still hear the voice under me, all round me, calling across from the bank. Not howling but soft. Come to me, it says. Come to me. I shut my eyes and the sun's shining on the lake and this time he stands and waits, he isn't going away. He shrugs the guitar behind him and squats down and puts his hand out to pull me in. And I swim, cutting waves in the water, getting closer, nearly at the other side.

I'm here, I say. I'm here.

Paul J. Martin

Art Zoo

Before I'd even brewed coffee that morning visitors to my gallery included a local homeless guy offering a cold kebab in exchange for one of my paintings...a Rasta with dusty grey dreads shrouded in dope smoke asking for a light...an elderly woman pushing a dachshund in a pram demanding shelter from the rain...

...And the two police officers who did me a favour by ruining my day.

Before any of that I'd made it through a night of strong weed and limp sex with the man who had made an uncomfortable habit of proposing. We'd made love, smoked some more, binged on chocolate cake, argued, made up and witnessed the sun rise too early.

He was sitting up in bed wrapped in my red silk kimono checking his phone while I was getting dressed and going heavy on the eye shadow and red lipstick. 'Listen,' he said, turning his attention to me, 'I'm so, so sorry. I've been bad.' He stuttered like a confession was on his lips.

'Eric, what's wrong?' In my mirror I saw him weeping and chewing his bottom lip – a sure sign he'd popped a pill when I'd not been paying attention. He glanced first at the plastic baggie he'd placed on the bedside cabinet then back at me. 'Forgive me. You're still the most important person in my life.'

'Still?' I asked. There was something new about this kind of pleading but I had no time for yet another heart-to-heart. I opened my gallery at ten.

I had no interest in class A drugs, no need of speed to define my purpose or provide misguided motivation. I was enjoying new responsibilities beyond our two bloated goldfish and my evening call-centre job selling insurance renewals to the ungrateful. The gallery was my dream, my baby, my creative road to independence. No way could my art project fail.

Before I'd moved in with Eric, he too had been creative, freelancing as a magician and making good money from an impressive catalogue of illusions he'd developed. He'd mesmerised packed theatres and wowed celebrities at fancy media events until some vindictive soul sussed his greatest feat of making small crowds vanish without trace. A YouTube video explaining his methods went viral and hey presto!.. his career disappeared in a flash. After months of unemployment and my footing the bills his best attempt at finding work had been snitching my Visa to print business cards promoting himself under a whole new name, claiming he was Magic Circle and yet still he had no gigs.

I gathered my bag, keys and nicotine gum while he ranted on about taking me away, renting a villa by the sea, enjoying gourmet dinners and vintage wines far away from his dealer who only came knocking when I was gone.

'Sounds lovely,' I said, not believing a word, 'and who's going to magic the money?'

He shrugged, 'I know I've been bad.' Sitting on the edge of the bed I was fastening my shoes as he spoke of a life that could be ours: nice country house, fancy cars and kids, lots of kids. I had already wasted so many tears arguing how this period of my life was for me, to progress my career as an artist and that kids figured nowhere in my plans. Regardless, he continued, 'Let's see,' now sniggering at nothing in particular, 'what could we call them...?' I buttoned up my coat while he smiled at reflections on the ceiling, reeling off strings of random names. 'Vincent, Rose, Lucy...Barney. Love Barney.'

That's when he lost me.

The pill had hijacked his brain.

Once again, I hated who he could be.

Too tired to drive, I braved the rain and boarded a crowded bus to the gallery. Sitting eyes closed with my head in my hands, I was afraid the vehicle's lurching and the stench of sodden human cargo would make me retch. I felt I could see through my eyelids, glimpsing a life wasted, a darkness that just got darker, Eric chasing after me, lost in an ever swelling crowd. The bus braked hard by my stop.

After the dachshund lady had left the gallery I was balancing on top of my step-ladder, hanging a painting while listening to music on my headphones - oblivious to the police walking in. They showed up like ghouls out of nowhere. What do you say when confronted by the law? No point in polite conversation. They're not your new best friends and they weren't there to make a purchase. I removed my headphones, placed them like a yoke around my neck and began a shaky descent. From the earnest looks on their faces this was no social visit. The WPC lifted her rain-spotted cap and ran her palm down her short ponytail. She forged a warm smile while her bearded colleague's blue eyes tried probing mine in search of an unknown truth.

The WPC nodded towards the hammer in my hand. 'Please, place that on the counter top. This won't take long.'

They had received complaints.

'About my work? Who from?'

'Not your work,' she said. 'It's about what you're selling, especially when sitting in the window.'

High in the bay window hung my custom-made red neon sign proclaiming Art Zoo and signage along the bottom of the window indicated my phone number, opening hours and the words, 'Or By Appointment'. In the bay stood the paint-splattered table covered in a deliberate chaos: squeezed tubes of coloured acrylics, brushes in jam jars, a small vase of drooping pink fuchsias and a vertical canvas on my easel – textured abstract in various shades of yellow. 'What I do when sitting in the window?' I asked. 'I perch on my stool and paint. What do you think?'

Then it hit me. 'Oh Jesus...!'

I was already regretting my choice of make-up.
The bearded officer scribbled notes in a small pad while his colleague leaned in close to the painting. 'Did *you* do this?' she asked, letting slip her professional facade and hinting at genuine interest. At that time of the morning I should have been drinking coffee and progressing my work, not wasting my time with police. Their visit was testing my patience.

'Yup,' I said, 'every bit.'

'Anyone else work here?'

'Just me.' Not entirely true. When I first collected the keys to the store it stank of cat piss and wet straw. Eric helped sand years of caked parrot poop off the wooden floors and disinfect the place throughout. We whitewashed the walls, installed new spotlights and polished the windows to a sparkle. Then we hung my work, my first ever one-woman show, where, on the opening night, people lined up along what had always been an unremarkable street, almost bringing traffic to a halt. After that, when neither booze nor drugs were flowing through his veins Eric was keen to man the gallery in the evening while I worked at the call-centre selling insurance. He enjoyed it, he said, got him out, helped meet new people.

The WPC stepped back from the painting.

'Huh...beautiful.'

'Mind if I hang my Open sign on the door?' I said, 'Saturday's my busiest day.'

Looking up from his notes the officer asked, 'By busy you mean?'

Before I could respond, the WPC asked, 'How do you know what to charge?' It's the question visitors asked most. Her colleague failed to hide a smug smile that smacked of loathing and distrust. He looked like he was stifling a sarcastic tirade. We shared an instant dislike.

I offered my standard reply. 'The price reflects my time, materials and what that work means to me.'

'Your time...,' repeated the officer, scratching his beard before making further notes. He sidled into the bay to check my work in progress. 'So,' he said, examining the cushioned seat of my stool, 'you sit here in the window? You, alone. Nobody else? No gentlemen, no other ladies...just you painting? Nothing else?'

'Just me. Painting, smudging, spraying, splashing. That's how I work. People stop to watch. I smile and wave, and encourage them to come in. We chat, I answer their questions and I hope they part with their cash...' As an afterthought I added, '...to buy a painting.'

The officer looked from the easel to the street where curious drivers peered in as they slowed for the traffic light which bathed the gallery walls in cranberry red, yielding to yellow and emerald green. The PC stepped out into the rain and looked back through the bay window before speaking into the device on his shoulder. His colleague peered behind the makeshift tweed curtain that separated the small rear kitchen from the gallery. She seemed satisfied there was nothing of interest: a tartan up-cycled love seat retrieved from a skip, the stainless-steel sink, electric kettle, coffee mugs, used dishcloths and my unsold paintings stacked against the wall. She turned to leave then stopped. Hooking her index finger like she was about to tickle my chin she gestured for me to join her. Pointing at four used condoms in the waste bin beside the sink she said, 'Madame, would you care to explain?'

Honestly?

I had no fucking clue.

The police station wasted most of my day. It wasn't the questioning that took time, rather the new investigating officers waiting for an interview room to come free after what I hoped were inquiries into more serious cases. I tried hard not to yell with frustration – with the police, whoever had filed the complaints and of course...with Eric. No wonder he enjoyed manning the gallery when I wasn't there. I dwelled on his deceit, the unanswered questions as well as that morning's attempts at his possible confession which I thought related to drugs. We had kept his amphetamine problems a secret, our personal omerta, but if the issue arose during questioning I felt poised to tell all.

Two detectives seated me at a metal table in a stark windowless room that reeked of bleach and fear.

They offered legal representation.

I declined.

My interview began under caution. The complaints, they said, talked of neighbours witnessing lurid goings-on in the gallery on more than one occasion. They asked about gallery opening hours, any private consultations and of course, Eric. When he helped, what he did there and for how long? Possible accusations, they explained, included public indecency, pandering and running a brothel. 'That's crazy,' I laughed. They stared at me unflinching. I kept repeating, 'This is bullshit! What the fuck?'

'Look,' I said, 'I'm selling paintings, nothing else. I call it Art Zoo. It's like performance art. When I have an audience I'm no longer working alone. Buyers can take home a painting they've seen evolving.' I worried I was saying too much. 'It's like witnessing the birth of a child. The work becomes personal to them. It carries a story they can share and it'll mean so much more.' I felt my words seep through the cracks in the walls. I wished I could do the same.

The lead investigator leaned back in his chair with his hands behind his shaved head smudging small bloody nicks on his scalp. 'Go on.'

'I might sit there looking like a caged animal but, as an artist who's used to working in a studio alone, it's liberating. The window offers light, appeals to my love of colour and it provides an occasional audience which inspires me every day. Plus, bottom line, I sell more.'

After endless paperwork they released me into what felt like a strange world of No. No charge against me, no apology, no let-up in the rain, no offer of a ride and, when I made a call sheltering from the storm beneath the station's overflowing gutters, no answer from Eric. I counted nine rings before hanging up. I wasn't even sure what I wanted from him - confessions, explanations, apologies or denials. Not denials. He owed me better lies than that. I bought my first pack of cigarettes in months and, beneath the dripping awning of a high street cafe, chain-smoked and sipped steaming coffee.

The heavy rain persisted as I walked for a good hour back to the gallery, hiding from passers-by behind my long sodden hair. People I did glimpse seemed heedless and mean. I wanted to muster anger, a visceral rage and rail at Eric face to face. Instead I was consumed by a numbing bewilderment, experiencing a zen-like state of inner silence, a delusive and misplaced peace.

Outside the gallery the unrelenting storm had plunged the street into a premature darkness, broken only by the headlights of passing vehicles. Stepping over the day's mail I locked the door behind me. In the kitchen I took a used tea towel to dry my face and hair. Hanging my wet coat on the hook above the waste-bin I noticed the offending condoms had been removed. Police evidence, I assumed. Sitting cross-legged in my love seat, I drank cold coffee and failed to find even a semblance of forgiveness for the man who had almost captured my heart. I sought solace in tears but they failed me. What I did was sit alone waiting; waiting for his call, waiting for excuses, his meaningless apologies, but most of all... waiting for the courage to move on.

The sharp snapping shut of the gallery's letter box is what woke me. In the darkness, softened only by the persistent alternating glow of the traffic lights, I made my way to the front door and retrieved what looked like junk mail and pizza coupons spread across the welcome mat. On top of the mail I found a handwritten note scribbled in thick black marker across a grubby envelope saying, Whore!

The ire I'd failed to muster earlier that day consumed every nerve in my body. Obliging tears blurred my vision. How had I got to this point when my sole aim was to succeed as an artist? From the bay window I looked out onto the stillness of the dark wet street. Among the flats opposite I saw a light going on behind a first-floor window, the nets moved and the lights went out.

Overwhelmed by an unusual sense of loneliness I succumbed to the niggling need to check Eric was at least okay.

After twelve rings he picked up.

No 'Hello.'

No 'Where have you been?'

No 'Are you okay?'

Just, 'Babe, you're fucking with my high.'

In the background I heard a woman's raspy voice, I guessed his dealer, calling out, 'Who the hell's that?'

That's when he lost me for good.

The gallery became my sanctuary for the night, my refuge from an onslaught of madness I had neither expected nor deserved. But instead of cowering behind the tweed curtain, dwelling in a quagmire of resentment, I switched on the red neon Art Zoo sign as well as the single spotlight which illuminated nothing but my easel, my painting and me. Perching myself upon the stool I took a palette knife, heaping thick swathes of various yellows upon the canvas.

I stared at the painting until it stared right back.

My tears I smudged into swirls of deep crimson. Contemplating my recent past I used a can of blue spray-paint to add a hasty blur of Eric's initials. Then I changed my mind, smearing the letters into the canvas with a dirty rag. I leaned back from the painting, alone but confidant, seeing the emergence of a powerful new work and glimpsing possibilities of which I'd been wholly unaware. With the palette knife I made a slash across the canvas, a cathartic release.

I can't recall how long I sat there, contemplating nothing but my new work. Thirty minutes, an hour maybe. Perhaps more. Eventually I rose from the stool, left the painting glowing beneath the spotlight for all passers-by to see then returned to the comfort of my love seat behind the tweed curtain, covering myself in the peculiar security of my damp coat.

The following morning I woke up chilly and stiff. There were no thoughts, no plans, not even disillusionment. I seemed unable to feel much of anything. While my coffee brewed I heard a knocking at the gallery door and stepped past the tweed curtain, dishevelled but happy not to care. The Rasta guy was shielding his eyes peering through the front door with his nose pressed to the glass. As I approached he smiled, revealing tobacco stained teeth. He pointed first at my painting on the easel nodding and giving me an approving thumbs-up then he pointed at the sign in my door which still said Open. Before I could find my keys to unlock the door he was making his way down the street.

Douglas Hill

Swimming Lessons

I was nearly 11 years old. I laughed like a girl, I looked like a girl, everyone said so. Now with my mother gone (cancer), my old man charged himself with shaping a boyhood for me. For a while it was his mission. Put your shoulders back, he said; stop feeling sorry for yourself; go outside and play with the other kids. He was not unduly harsh, or cruel, just inexperienced. We ate a lot of pizza. He invited me to sit and watch the rugby with him, bribing me with beer shandy. He fed me paperbacks by Wilbur Smith and Ernest Hemingway. He had loads of them. The Hemingway books were yellow with age or being in the sun and there was ash trapped between the pages. Where'd these come from, I wanted to know. From your *oupa*, he said, who passed them on to me; now they're yours. The short stories about boys fishing, first love and heartbreak, and sleeping out under the stars in Michigan were okay. It was the ones about bullfighting I didn't get. The only thing I liked about them was the matadors' 'suit of lights'. The tight blue pants were cool, the shiny black pumps, the square shoulders and brocade of the tiny jacket, and the hat - the montera. When I mentioned this, my old man asked if I'd read the one about Frances Macomber and how he stood his ground and shot the charging lion. I said it was cruel to kill such a noble beast. He shook his head. He may have cursed under his breath. A free swearer usually, he was trying to tone it down in his role as sole parent. Instead of the f-word, he used milder expletives. He didn't use any Afrikaans swear words, although there are some good ones, some real dirty ones that are as obscene as the oaths the matadors used although not as long or as insulting about one's mother. He'd also stopped drinking every day. He was already pretty old, in his 40s, when they had me, their only child. They liked to tell me about all the years they had tried for a baby and how they'd all but given up (too much information) until I appeared, the Miracle Bean. I loved my father; he was all I had and I knew he was trying to steel me for the stuff I'd have to face in life, but I wished he had something else. So, although it was only a few months after my mother died, I was glad when he met Teresa.

It was on the night of his company's annual dinner when all the staff from the different branches got together and awards were handed out. My old man hadn't wanted to go but as sales manager he had to be there. He must have asked me ten times if I'd be okay on my own. I won't be late, I'll be back by 11, he promised, before driving off. It was after 3 in the morning when I heard the sound of voices. There was whispering and some giggling but after a while it went quiet. I must have gone back to sleep until I was woken up again by the noises coming from the bedroom.

I don't want to say it was the first thing I noticed about Teresa and that it was more to do with the fact that she was with my father, with someone my father's age, and that she was wearing one of his shirts and had nothing on underneath and that she was in our home at breakfast time smelling of perfume and had glitter in her hair, than the fact that she was Cape Coloured or maybe Cape Malay. At school they told us not to label people by colour anymore although my old man's generation did it all the time still. When he introduced us, he watched to see how I'd react, if I'd take it as some kind of affront to my mother's memory etc., but I was friendly, I said hello. Later, I found out she was a dancer and was one of the performers at a club my old man and some of the other car salesmen had gone to after their company night.

'Is Teresa living here now?' I said, after she'd been

there every morning for over a week.

'Would you mind if she was?'

I shrugged. It wasn't as if she tried to tell me what to do. When she said Ryan was a funny name for a girl and realised her mistake, she just laughed it off. She was kind of flirty and credited me with more than I knew, which I liked. They went out nearly every night to where she danced at this gentleman's club and they'd still be in bed when I got up for school in the morning. I got used to seeing her stuff lying about, her skimpy things, bright and shrivelled up like burst balloons on the floor, and her brown skin against the white of the sheets while the old man lay with his arm over his eyes, lined and tired in sleep. I'd help myself to money from his trousers which he hung over the bedroom door. For a while, every night was a party night.

*

A few of weeks after Teresa moved in, I was coming up the path from school when I saw the neighbour, Mr Ackerman, standing by the hedge that divided our properties. Mr Ackerman operated one of the big cranes at the docks and spent all day in his little cabin. He liked it up there, looking down on everyone. He told us about the important work he did, loading and unloading cargo from the holds of ships with all the stuff people wanted: computers, laptops, mobile phones, flatpack furniture. He drove a *bakkie* with 'Smooth Operator' stencilled on the driver's door. In the afternoons, when he got home from work, he sat on his stoep in the shade drinking brandy and Coke. It looked like he was just passing time until he could get back to his crane and away from life at ground level. He was about the same age as my old man but they'd had a falling out over a car a few months earlier and weren't talking, although he was still talking to me apparently.

'Hey funny one.'

'What?' I knew he only wanted to get me talking because the sound of my voice amused him.

He was dangling a chameleon between his two fingers. So what? There were lots of them living in the greenery. 'Check this out,' he said. He put his head back and slowly lowered the chameleon into his open mouth then closed it. He hummed and rolled his eyes and tapped his watch, signalling me to wait. When he pulled the chameleon out again it had turned a light shade of brown.

I nodded to show I was impressed, and so I could go.

'Here's one for you,' he said, 'how many chameleons you reckon got into the ark?' But before I could answer, he said: 'Who knows?' He waited to see if I got it. Then he dropped the chameleon onto the hedge where it stayed, one foot suspended in mid-air, before starting to move off in slow motion, rolling its eyes to look at us as if to say, now what? Gradually it changed back to green until it merged with the bush and disappeared.

'See your dad's got himself a girlfriend,' Mr Ackerman said.

I shrugged.

'At first, I thought maybe you'd got a maid.'

'She's not a maid.'

'I hear you. She doesn't look like one, that's for sure. In our day that kind of thing was hidden but not anymore. Now it's your day, eh?'

Again, I shrugged.

'Anyway, it's a good party trick but it leaves a bad taste in the mouth. I wouldn't try it if I were you.'

'What?'

He cleared his throat and spat on the ground. 'Chameleons.'

*

I was doing homework at the kitchen table when I heard the door going and then the old man came in. I waited for Teresa to appear behind him but he was on his own. He tossed his car keys onto the worktop.

'What's wrong?' I said.

'Nothing, why?'

'You're back early.'

He pointed at the half-eaten pack of Sweetie Pies on the table. 'Tell me that wasn't your supper.'

'I had the *bobotie* Teresa made. Where is she?'

'At work.'

'Is something wrong?'

'You just asked me that.'

'The *bobotie*'s still warm if you want some.'

He glanced at the dish on top of the cooker and shook his head. 'I thought we'd go swimming.'

The fact that I couldn't swim really bothered him. He'd given up on trying to get me interested in rugby but it was as if no real progress could be made until I'd mastered the front crawl or at least breaststroke. You can't do doggy paddle for the rest of your life, he said. Who says I have to go in the water anyway, I countered. Everyone does in this country, he said, which I took to mean everyone went in the water which wasn't actually true. My mother hadn't been wild about swimming either. Splashing herself with water to cool down from time to time was enough for her; she preferred sunbathing, although her skin just went red and then she'd start to peel. She used to moan about not being able to get any colour, despite trying all the different oils and lotions. After a few months of chemo when all her hair had fallen out, her skin took on a golden-like glow.

Finally, she said: a tan.

I'd heard Teresa and the old man come in around two but instead of going straight to bed as usual (cue time to put my head under the pillow), they went through to the kitchen where they carried on talking.

'Ok, but why a cruise liner?' I heard him say.

'Because it's better paid and it's real dancing, there are routines to learn. There's a choreographer. I'd be part of a troupe.'

'Is that who interviewed you, the choreographer?'

'Auditioned me, yes. His name is Raoul.'

'What did Raoul get you to do?' my old man said.

'Dance, what do you think? Don't look at me like that, Archie.'

'Like what?'

'You know.'

'So how long are these cruises?'

'Six weeks.'

'Six weeks?'

'Maybe longer, depending on the itinerary. Anyway, I probably won't get it.'

The old man cleared his throat. 'What about me? I mean, I thought we…'

'Go on, Archie, I'm listening.'

I was listening too but I didn't hear what he said, if he said anything at all and everything went quiet until the silence was broken by the sound of a match being struck. After a while a chair scraped on the floor and someone got up and went through to the bathroom. The light in the kitchen stayed on for another ten minutes or so until whoever was in there must have got tired because the light went out and a moment later I heard the bedroom door closing.

*

The old man was driving one of the new demonstrators – the latest Audi – which was completely soundproof. The dry country rushed past like a virtual landscape, without so much as a whisper. Teresa was looking out the window; what at, only she knew. She'd hardly said a word since we left. She was smoking which my old man didn't like in the car, but he didn't say anything. He even offered her the car lighter to light her cigarette, but she insisted on using a match from one of the little matchbooks she got from the club where she worked, even though it took about three before one would fire. It was my 11th birthday and we were heading for some place up the coast, on the Indian Ocean side. It was a long way and the first time the three of us had gone anywhere together. It felt a bit weird.

'Why come all this way just for a swim?' Teresa said, after another few kilometres had passed in silence.

'This is a good spot. There's a big rock pool. We'll have the place to ourselves.'

'Oh, I see.'

'What's that supposed to mean?'

'Just forget it.'

Ten minutes later, we slowed down to turn off at a sign for Hook Bay.

'Here?' said Teresa, sitting up. 'Isn't this where that woman was killed by a shark?' She looked all around, as if there'd still be blood or some other sign this was the spot where it had happened, but the old man was too busy trying to avoid potholes in the dirt road to say anything. Finally, we stopped at a headland overlooking a small bay. He got out and lit a cigarette while dust from the road slowly settled around us.

'It *was* here wasn't it? Why here of all places?'

'That woman was swimming out in the bay. We'll be in the rock pool – no sharks will come in there.'

'I won't be in anywhere.'

He shook his head.

'Don't tell me you're surprised?'

He leaned in to look at me in the back seat.

'Today's the day, little man.'

'Go ahead, feed your son to the sharks,' said Teresa.

My old man winked, waiting for me to say something. 'We came all this way, Ryan.'

'I know.'

'You can swim in the rock pool. It'll be safe.'

'Safe,' said Teresa.

We carried our stuff down the steep path to a flat area above the rock pool where my old man spread out the blanket, getting down on his hands and knees to feel for stones. He stripped off and jumped straight into the pool, making a big splash of it: *see, this is how you do it.* He dived under, showing his backside, and came up blowing and holding a handful of kelp, slick like a bunch of entrails he'd ripped from the belly of something down there.

'All clear,' he said, after heaving the kelp into the open sea.

I squatted on the rocks above him, arms round my knees

'What you so miserable about?' he said.

'I'm not.'

'You're 11 years old Ryan. I'd been swimming for five years at your age.'

'I don't blame him,' said Teresa.

'That's right, encourage him, why don't you?'

'Come for a walk, Ryan,' Teresa said.

'I don't want to.'

'Suit yourself.' She got to her feet. I tried not to watch, but it was impossible. Eyes were drawn to her like iron filings to a magnet when she walked. It made you stop whatever else you were doing. And she walked knowing she was being watched, like a catwalk model. My old man was standing in the rock pool, statue-like, his hair plastered to his head and his bald spot showing through.

'Don't worry about it,' he said as Teresa started up the path, brown and long-legged in the sun in her yellow bikini.

'I'm not worried.'

'Good. How about a swim?'

'Not just now, maybe later.'

'The water's warm. Feel it.'

'I believe you.'

'It's the Indian Ocean. Can you smell it?'

I nodded. It smelled like ink, or watercolour paint. Or blood.

'Is it safe?' I said.

'Of course it is. I'll stay in with you if you like.'

'Not the water, I mean up there.'

'Oh.'

Teresa was standing on top of the cliff, right at the edge it seemed, looking out to sea. I waved up to her but she didn't wave back. Someone else appeared on the cliff, carrying a surfboard. She must have said something because he stopped and put the board down. They stood there talking, the surfer's long hair blowing out tangled in the wind. We saw Teresa put a hand on his shoulder and lean in close, holding her hair away from her face. The strange sound of her laughter carried down to us at the rock pool. My old man was squinting up at them and for the first time it struck me that one day his strength would peter out, his body fail him. His lifespan was finite, just like everyone else's.

*

'Is that what you're into now?' he said when Teresa came back, half an hour later.

'What are you talking about?'

'We saw the surfer chatting you up, didn't we, Ryan?'

'So you're spying on me?'

'We heard you laughing - what was the big joke?'

'I couldn't get a match to work.'

'Yeah, how's that funny?'

'God, Archie.' She started to rub oil on her arms.

'Did you ask surfer boy about the sharks?' he said.

'As a matter of fact, I did. He said they sometimes see them when they're out on their boards.'

'But it doesn't stop him?'

She shrugged: 'He says the surf's good.'

She handed me the oil: 'Do my neck, please Ryan.'

She put her head forward and lifted her hair to expose her long neck, just like Mary Queen of Scots did. First, she pardoned her executioner who stood by with his axe until she was ready and then he took two blows to behead her. *So perish all the Queen's enemies*, he said to the crowd, holding up her dripping head.

We got it in History.

When I finished, Teresa put on her sunglasses and lay on her side on the blanket and started to flick through a magazine. My old man opened a *dinkie* of beer and drank it down in one go.

'Are you just going to lie there all day?' he said.

Teresa stayed silent behind her big glasses. He tossed the bottle aside and lowered himself into the pool. He kicked his way over to the gap in the rocks where the sea came in then ducked under the next swell. The white length of him shot out between the rocks into the open sea. He started swimming into the bay, the suck of the tide taking him out so that soon he was a long way from the rocks. The water was clear enough to see his feet and even the cord on his red trunks as he swam further out. When he was in the middle of the bay, 100 yards or more from the rocks, he stopped to tread water and wave back, crossing his arms above his head the way people do when they want rescued. I studied the sea around him. As the old man rose and fell in the glassy swells with his puny legs kicking away beneath him, I kept seeing the fin of a shark fizzing the surface or the dark shadow of one gliding silently underwater, a great white or a Zambezi. I climbed higher on to the rocks so I could see more. No one could outswim a shark and there wasn't a buoy or anything for him to hold on to out there.

'What's the matter?' said Teresa

'He's way out in the middle.'

She sat up, using the magazine to shield her eyes. 'What's he trying to prove?'

I cupped my hands and shouted at him to come back but my voice got swallowed up in the wind and sound of the waves crashing.

*

My hands were shaking so much it took two matches to light his cigarette.

'Thanks,' he said when I passed it down to him. The muscles in his leg were still twitching and every now and then a shudder went through him. Beads of water trembled on his ears and the tip of his nose. He was staring hard into the pool, with his feet dangling in the water.

I gave him a towel to dry his hands and face.

'I'll go in next time,' I said.

'Okay.'

'I don't feel like it today.'

'It's okay, Ryan.'

'I've got a sharp pain. I think it's my heart.'

My old man smiled. 'Your heart?'

'Here,' I said, pressing.

'That's more like your stomach.'

'It's in that area,' I said.

There was the sound of scrabbling above us. Teresa, who'd been lying there, long faced and serious, sat up and whipped off her glasses: 'For God's sake Ryan, go in or don't go in, but stop making excuses. You said you weren't scared of the water any more. You said you'd jump in. Don't be such a *mophie*. I bet you'll still want something on the way back.'

'I don't want anything.'

'Do you hear that, Archie?'

'Leave him alone, okay? And don't call him that.'

'Well, it's time he stopped acting like one.'

I got to my feet. I felt the rush of air on my skin and in the next instant, the cold crush of the water. There was another splash and when I opened my eyes the old man was next to me in the rock pool, his grinning face inches away.

'I knew you could do it.'

All the heaviness had left me. All the tightness had gone from the place where it hurt. I swam the length of the pool, turned and swam back again, burying my face in the water and turning my arms over. I front-crawled up and down while the old man got out to watch from the rocks.

'I'm swimming,' I shouted to Teresa, all loathing for her forgotten. She hadn't got the job as a dancer on the cruise liner just like she'd predicted, although I knew she said it in the hope of being proved wrong in the way we sometimes ask for things. She's going to die, isn't she? I'd said to the old man, seeing my mother shrunk to bones overnight and suddenly old; wanting him to be able to say, no, she's not, although I already knew what the answer was.

'Come in,' I said, but Teresa acted as if she didn't hear me. She lit another cigarette with one of her iffy matches and lay back on the towel. I don't know if by then she'd already decided she was going to leave us. I don't know if she had it all planned out. She was probably still to decide for definite but I don't know what, if anything, would have changed her mind. Twice over we'd proved our braveness to her, but it didn't make any difference in the end.

Tanvir Bush

Rictus

Doctor Elias Banda sits on the porch at the back of his living quarters in an old and very comfortable canvas strap chair. He is reading a book of short stories by Chekhov in the original Russian, mouthing the words aloud to himself with great pleasure. He has taken off his shirt and sandals, letting his stomach relax and expand over the belt of his shorts; a bottle of warm beer sits between his bare feet. The heat is stupefying. Sweat beads glint at his hair line and his fingers stick to the pages of the book leaving slight smudges in the ink.

The little concrete porch is built into the hill, its tin roof poking out into the thick bush that covers the pink, brittle, rock of the hill face. Creepers twine lazily around the roof poles slinging themselves, like a huge tapestry, over the top and down the sides of the porch, shading it almost completely. Things slither within the tendrils; lizards and tiny birds, insects, mice, bats and snakes but the overall cooling effect is much coveted by the other hospital staff and especially the English volunteer, Dennis, who suffers loudly from heat rash.

The far end of the terrace looks out over the valley and down to the little town with its tin roofs shimmering in the October heat. It is the dry season and dust has climbed into the very tops of the trees. Everything is parched and absolutely still with only the constant high-pitched, zinging song of the cicadas ringing like tinnitus. October is known in almost all of Zambia's different dialects as the 'month of madness' and Elias strongly suspects this has something to do with the cicadas' endless electronic shriek.

He brushes away a couple of flies from the top of his bottle before taking a swig. He hates warm beer but the electricity has gone down again, the ancient generator spluttering to silence for the third time this month. Jonas has gone off in the battered pick-up to find the engineer and a spare part from town. Luckily, the hospital is quiet. The heat keeps many of the outpatients panting in the cool of their huts and shacks. Of the twenty beds only six are occupied and all are palliative care; end-stage AIDS cases flitting between consciousness and coma. When the power had gone down Elias had conscripted Dennis and they had managed to seal the fridges as best as they could to protect the last of the blood, pharmaceuticals and lab supplies but the beer was not a priority and as a consequence, is warm.

'Ya paneemayoo,' Elias reads out loud to a particularly astonished looking gecko that clings with its padded feet to the roof pole. In the book a Russian doctor tells a mental patient that he understands him when patently he does not. Elias tuts at the page, shaking his head sagely. He studied medicine in Moscow, sent over on a government sponsorship at the end of the Cold War. His father, a Marxist academic teaching at the University of Lusaka was beside himself with pride. That had been twenty years ago; before Elias acquired his two wives and their endless parasitic extended families. Now he had abandoned them all and his successful practice in Lusaka, escaping here to the Hilltop Catholic Mission Hospital ostensibly to study malarial resistance in the local community. Initially it had been a great relief to have quiet and time to study and read. But now Elias, sitting in the bone crushing heat in the middle of the African bush, remembers Moscow in winter; the ice on the trees, the smoke of breath. He seems to smell the white spirit of the chilly, teaching hospital, *ahhh… the breasts of those nurses.* How he longed to return there….Moscow!

He is shaken from his reverie by the faint sound of

an engine and people shouting. Jonas must be getting back with the engineer. *At last*, thinks Elias and anyway it is about time he checked on old Sister Michael and that useless waste of space Dennis in the lab. Grudgingly, he replaces his bookmark and stands up, sticking a finger down his shorts to pull his sweaty pants from the crack between his buttocks. Slipping on his sandals, not bothering with the heel straps, he plucks his damp shirt and white lab coat from where they dangle from the door frame.

From the staff quarters it is a quick, sun-blinding walk across the yard, scattering chickens and a few bleating goats, into the back of the hospital and through the near empty corridor to the front entrance and car park. Dennis and Sister Michael are already there and Elias notes the elderly Polish sister holds a wheelchair. He cocks his head towards it.

'Jonas radioed ahead, Doctor. They have someone in the back of the pick-up, a new admission,' she explains, pushing her round glasses up her button nose then turns her myopic gaze back to the road, anxiously crossing herself, her white habit gleaming. As always Elias wonders how she keeps so clean and cool under all that linen. Never even once has he seen even the smallest stain of blood or vomit on her apron, even after she has been grappling with a disorientated patient or managing a soiled bed change.

Dennis, on the other hand, is always grubby. He seems to have decided that being 'In Africa' allows him to be perpetually semi clad and unwashed. Today he wears a stained blue vest, red shorts and flip flops. Elias glances over at him. In the heat Dennis has become paler, patches of sun burn standing out like red paint on his oily skin, his small eyes narrowed to pinpricks against the white sunlight and his Adam's apple bob-

bob-bobbing in anticipation. Elias doesn't like Dennis's attitude; something to do with the way the young man talks about the mission hospital as 'my little bush clinic' even though he has only been in the country for three months.

The sound of the engine and the shouts of several voices grow louder and the pick-up appears over the crest of the hill and pulls up to the hospital gates in a cloud of red dust. The back of the vehicle is crowded. Three men and two women scramble down and begin to pull something from the bed of the truck. It looks like a body but it is unbending, stuck in the wrong shape; a stiff, unyielding arc like an upside-down canoe, covered with several pieces of cloth to protect it from the sun.

'Doesn't look like you'll be needing that,' says Elias winking at Sister Michael and the wheelchair and stepping out into the fray.

The patient is hefted through the hospital doors and into the single bedded emergency room where the body is lain on top of the gurney. The men stand back and the two women come forward and take off the covering cloths, Elias blinks, shocked.

The patient is a girl, a broad and heavy teenager, her face fat and stippled with acne. Her legs stick out straight in front of her and her arms hang loose and relaxed down at her sides but her back is completely bowed; only the very back of her head and her buttocks touch the mattress. Her position is physically imp-ossible, looks excruciating and yet here she is, breathing quietly with no sign of trauma. Immediately Elias tests her for tetanus but she has no fever. Her skin is cool and the muscles, although in spasm, are not dappled with built up lactic acid and there is no evidence of tearing of the tendons, in fact no torsion or swelling anywhere on her body. Elias feels strange. He feels a little afraid. The girl's eyes are almost shut, just a sliver of white glints from behind the lashes, and although her jaw is clenched firmly shut, her expression is peaceful, almost dreamy.

'What happened? Give me the facts,' he demands as he sweeps around the gurney, checking the girl's vitals. The men and woman crowd around, all talking at once. One of them shakes a newspaper angrily at the doctor but he cannot make out what they are saying. Elias is a city boy and although he speaks English, Russian, Nyanja, Bemba and a spattering of Mandarin, this village dialect is strange to him. He turns to Sister Michael who has been here at the Mission Hospital so long that her Polish is ebbing away, crowded out by all the different voices she has absorbed. She takes the villagers to one side. Dennis meantime, flapping about excitedly like an oversized fruit bat, is sent off with Jonas and the engineer to help fix the generator.

'A famous pastor from America came to their village ten days ago,' reports Sister Michael. She hands Elias the newspaper where the face of the Evangelist minister Jimmy Swells fills half the front page.

'So...?' asks Elias taking the girl's blood pressure for the third time. According to the monitor she is as good as dead, her heart-beat impossibly slow, her pressure critically low. He tries again. In a distant part of his mind he has a vague memory of the hospital staff talking excitedly about this Jimmy Swells. There had been a certain fanatical quality to the breathy whispers, rapture usually reserved for *Our Lord*.

'He came and preached at the central church in Londazo Province and for three days and nights everyone prayed and sang and danced. But the day he left, several young girls fainted into shapes like this one…' Sister Michael pauses, not quite indicating the girl on the table, not quite looking at her. 'The women lay like so for several days. They all recovered except for this one. Her name is Nandini.'

'Shapes like these.' Elias does the math. 'God! So she has been like this for a week? Ridiculous! Astounding!'

Sister Michael listens to some more of the villagers' hurried song-like speech. 'They have been pushing crushed banana between her teeth and given her water but yes…seven days.' Without thinking the Sister begins to intone a Hail Mary. Several of the villagers join in.

Elias squeezes her delicate shoulder affecting calm he does not feel. 'Now just stop that clap trap!' he chuckles, gesticulating wildly with a reflex hammer. 'That's what got this woman into this bloody mess in the first place. It's a hysterical response, nothing supernatural, Sister. I need you to take her family and fill in the admission forms, alright?'

Sister Michael hustles the villagers from the room, leaving Elias with the girl on the gurney. The body is preposterous. The woman looks as if she is falling through the air or dropping down in water. She should be soft and pliable. She is like rock. A sculpture of a girl falling. Is it a joke, a fake? Elias circles the gurney once, twice., touching her cool, dry, living skin, watching the tiny shine of white below her eyelids. After a moment, he throws the hammer at the wall. He has no idea what to do next.

It is Dennis who comes up with a treatment. He jogs, without knocking, into the room and whistles, impressed. 'Freak out, man!' he hisses, clapping Elias on the back. 'This is a good one!' For a while he watches the girl with his mouth wide open as if she were an exhibit in a fair. Then his face changes, his eyes become somehow even smaller.

'I have an idea…'

Elias, who is looking at his battered Gray's Anatomy textbook, ignores him.

Undeterred he comes close and Elias gets a waft of sweaty feet.

'We need to get them to believe our God… or rather our "doctor magic", is more powerful than the American pastor's,' Dennis hisses excitedly over Elias's shoulder. Behind the hospital. the generator roars briefly and then coughs and dies. Elias hears the duty nurses begin placing and lighting candles. Darkness is lapping at the edges of things, blurring faces. Elias blinks, wipes his mouth.

'It can't hurt after all,' Dennis cajoles. 'It would just be an experiment.'

'Just an experiment..?' mimics Elias bitterly. 'You are mocking these people!'

'Aw, come on Elias. You yourself told me the people around here were primitive and superstitious. "Hysteria" you always say, an "hysterical response", re-member? You, are man of science at the end of the day and….'

'Yes yes…but that is not the point here.' Elias can't express what he feels inside. He stares at the girl lying contorted, silent, barely breathing on the bed, and his heart judders as if he were being judged somehow, tested. A memory of his grandmother comes into his mind. She had been a gifted healer, well known for her ability with what he would call mental illness and what she had called 'possession. He had never even asked her about it, her use of herbs, her skill with diagnosis, her beliefs. She had died long before he took up medicine.

'Are you scared?' Dennis stands over him not bothering to mask his irritation. His breath is rotten and his tone imperious. 'You know even in Europe religious hysteria can cause the body to behave in extreme...'

'It's not that!' Elias snaps before Dennis can begin to lecture him on the fallibility of the human mind. 'It just seems so...' He flounders wanting to say 'rude', 'ignoble'; but instead puffs the words out between pursed lips without articulating them. He knows that Dennis could never grasp the complexity of the emotion he is grappling with, a combination of dread, shame, and sorrow. He shrugs, capitulates. He is at a loss. 'Okay, we will try your experiment.'.

Dennis brings extra candles into the emergency room and begins 'dressing his set' without letting on to Sister Michael who would *definitely* not approve. He raids the lab for beakers, test-tubes and an assortment of chemicals, becoming quite shrill as he bosses people around, bringing the girl's parents and two goggle-eyed nurses to stand one in each corner of the room. He insists on Elias dressing in his scrubs from head to foot, including a mask and a cap. Elias hadn't even known the hospital had any caps.

Elias has been given his instructions and although rather mortified at having allowed Dennis such control, part of him remains distant and removed, wondering if such an experiment might actually work. He knows the girl is exhibiting some kind of hysterical paralysis but he can't come to terms with the improbability of her body, her lack of pain, her stolid calm. He is furious with her, wanting to shake her. But those eyes... He is also still more than a little afraid.

Dennis is all knees and elbows, his Adam's apple bobbing as he drips chemicals into beakers and preps test tubes.

'It's time!' he calls dramatically and pushes the wheeled trolley of props over to where Elias is standing next to the girl on the gurney. In the gloom. Elias can see the whites of Nandini's eyes gleaming. Dennis dribbles something into the beakers of chemicals and white smoke, slowly at first and then faster and faster begins to pour out of the tops of the containers and onto the table. The nurses gasp and cover their mouths.

Dennis nods at Elias who rolls his eyes churlishly but begins crushing the paracetamol on the table in front of the girl. For added affect he intones, in Russian, the names of various parts of the body and Dennis smiles, pleased with Elias's improvisation. Carefully Elias sweeps the crushed white powder into two test tubes and fills them with distilled water. One he hands to Dennis who, solemn as a priest walks the room, giving a little sip to each of the audience in a rough styled communion. The other test tube Elias raises dramatically to the ceiling and after making a vague sign of the cross and thinking 'Holy Christ' to himself, leans over and pours into the girl's clenched jaws.

'Wake up Nandini!' he shouts.

At that very moment, the generator roars into life and the lights come on with a blinding fizz and a pop.

Everyone jumps and in the stark light of the emergency ward they eye each other, shocked and embarrassed. Elias takes off the ridiculous cap and wipes the sweat from his brow. He feels like an idiot. Pushing the table to one side he leans over the girl to check her vitals once more and she suddenly gasps, flops flat and lies on the bed with her eyes wide open.

From behind him Elias hears Dennis and the two nurses shout with triumph and amazement and the girl's family move in wailing joyfully.

The girl is fine. She has no back pain, no cramping. Her blood pressure is normal and she seems perfectly collected and rational. She says she had no memory of anything. She smiles and smiles at Dennis. There is something slightly distasteful to Elias about her expression. She looks to him as if she is smirking. Her relatives dance around her, trying to ply Sister Michael with well-used kwacha notes and clapping Elias and Dennis on the back over and over until Dennis's sunburn forces him to retreat to the common room with the giggling nurses.

Elias listens to the joyful singing and ululations of Nandini's family fading away with the 'phutt-phutt' of the Land Rover engine as Jonas drives them back down the hill.

Later, back on his dark cool porch, with the rustle of the tiny things all around him, Elias takes a swig of a fresh, now slightly chilled beer. He doesn't feel good about the incident. In fact, he still feels foolish and confused as if someone had played an almighty joke on him. He can imagine Dennis later on, back in England, telling everyone about 'the primitive hysteric' he had treated and he swallows, ashamed. There must have been a medical procedure he could have used. A nightjar shrieks and Elias twitches uneasily, listening to the darkness and imagining something monstrous and stealthy moving through the bush. He remembers his grandmother pouring maize beer onto the road one white-hot day, appeasing the spirits before his parents drove off to Lusaka. The tarmac had been baking, the beer had hissed and smoked.

'They prefer blood but you can distract them with beer.'

Had she said that to him, looking down, winking?

Half a century later, Elias looks at his own beer bottle, fearfully recalling the impossible position of Nandini's back. He wonders, tipping the beer and watching it fizz on the hot shadowed stone, what his grandmother would have done in his place.

Maureen Cullen

Isa's Pitch

The airmail letter rustled in Isa's pocket. Jean was doing so well in New York. She scolded Isa when she found out about the last pregnancy. And here she was telling her about this new pill that stopped a woman getting pregnant, no matter the time of the month. All you did was swallow a tablet. Isa took the midwife at the clinic aside and showed her the airmail, but she pooh-poohed it, said it was only to be given if a woman's health required it, and as Isa was fit as a bull this wasn't going to be possible.

All morning the boys had hung like rags over the furniture and across the landing. Now one was on his knees under the kitchen table scrambling for his dice, nearly tumbling the pile of Beanos and Dandys she'd laid out for them. Two were having a tournament to decide First Knight, throwing a spear made from a broom out the back door to roars of delight when it stuck in the tiny patch of wet grass. Trouble was they brought back mud every time they retrieved it. Someone would be black and blue before the afternoon ended. The noise was reaching pitch level but, thank God, now the smirr had stopped, she could send them outside to play. Isa sighed, eight long weeks of school holidays yet to go.

'Jamie, go get Connor and Liam, and put the shoes on wee Frank. Sam, get the baw fae the hut.'

Within minutes, five boys spilled out the front door screeching for their pals, leaving Isa to take a break at the kitchen table. The house seemed to exhale with their passing. Charlie crawled over to her feet and pulled himself up to her knee, velvet blue eyes begging for a cuddle. She hiked him up to her lap by the oxters and kissed the top of his silken head, lemon verbena tickling her nose. Ben had slept all through the commotion on his back in the pram, his chubby legs bent so that the knees pointed outwards, the soles of his feet pressed together. A bonny bairn, like the rest of them. A mistake, this time, although she'd never part with him.

She got to her feet, swinging Charlie onto her hip, his fingers clasped in her hair, and poured a cup of tea from the dented pot idling on the stove. They sat on the concrete doorstep, he sooking a lolly, she sipping bitter tea, while downhill at Havoc Shore, clouds scudded over the Clyde. The estate perched on the cliffside, and her back windows felt the strain of the wind and water that drenched the town in the harsh winters, but in the summertime the views were resplendent, the skies a constantly moving panoply of light. Isa savoured this moment of peace, before the bairn woke, or two of them came back before the others, one hurt, the other supervising the return of the casualty, the wail a siren screech as the injured party was guided by the elbow up the hill.

The sky lightened as she sat, clouds thinning and patches of blue forming just before the sun slid out and winked at them, picking out the blackcurrant streaks on Charlie's face as he scrunched his eyes against the glare. The grass began to dry, the heat causing mist to rise in a sheet, droplets glistening like a carpet of diamonds. Those steaming nappies could come off the pulley and be hung out, but she'd wait a few minutes as the weather today was full of devilment.

Two still in nappies. She flushed with irritation every time Angus joked he was raising a fitbaw team. He knew how much she wanted a daughter and he was willing to keep going until that happened, but she wasn't willing to risk more pregnancies. She'd followed Doctor Sloan's advice but it hadn't worked. Out popped Ben in full throttle, number seven on Angus' team list. No delicate wee lass to dress up, no pigtails to plait, no dance classes, no companion for her middle years.

That midwife had a cheek. Isa wouldn't be fit as a bull for much longer if this went on. She'd end up like her poor mother, dead at fifty, her heart swollen after fourteen pregnancies, six of them not surviving the birth or the first weeks of life. Isa hugged the little one next to her. She'd birthed eight, the lost one a steel band around her heart to this day. No, she didn't want to end up an old woman before her time, breathless, wrinkled, fussing over false teeth, her calcium reserves all used up. Isa shivered. That awful day at the dentist, Isa let off school so she could offer her mum a guiding arm home after the extractions. The pervasive smell of gas, Mum's ghastly face, her mouth dripping blood. No, enough was enough.

Though how she'd pitch that one to Angus, she didn't know. He followed the priest to the letter. Father Jim, after belching out Frankincense and Myrrh on the altar, apoplectic on the pulpit about the rise of contraception and the fall of grace. She smiled, he hadn't heard the grunts and fidgeting in the pews on the women's side of the chapel. Isa'd asked her pal, Lizzie, who'd been to university, all about it, and she said The Pill was legal for married women and not to listen to the midwife. Lizzie talked about women's liberation and something called The New Wave, and gave her a book by Sylvia Plath, but Isa hadn't been able to make head nor tail of that.

She heard the boys before she saw them, but they'd only been gone twenty minutes, and no one was wailing. She perked her ears to a swell of excited chatter interrupted by a whistle's peep, picked up Charlie and hurried to the front gate. They were piling up the brae, her own five with seven or more of the others, enough for six-a-side and a ref who was giving it laldy on his whistle, while two headed the baw back and forth as they went.

Jamie ran on towards her. 'Mam, Mam.'

The boys crowded around, Connor squeezing through to stand on the bar and swing the gate, eyes stuck on Isa's face.

The bigger boys wore an expression of disgusted disbelief. The last time Isa saw that on her oldest son's face was when Charlie's nappy leaked over Jamie's Celtic strip while they played keepie-uppie, the bairn balanced on the soles of his big brother's feet. The excitement had caused a blast of excrement that would fill a cowshed.

'They've shut the pitch doon.'

This echoed through the crowd, repeated by every boy in turn.

'Aye, closed big gates.'

'Big sign up.'

'We couldnae get in.'

'Aye they've shut us oot.'

Shut us oot was wailed forth like the chorus of a choir, but these were no choirboys. Jamie's hair aye stuck up like straw, no matter how many combs she broke on it. Her Jamie was the grubbiest boy on the estate, his knees aye scraped and bleeding - he could trip over a ten-ton boulder he could - and wee Frank couldn't keep that tongue behind his lips, it hung out like a spaniel's. The other boys were a ragtag bag of soiled arms, legs and mugs, those mugs silent now, registering their collective outrage, waiting for her response, the only sound the regular squeak of the gate's hinges.

'Whit does the sign say?'

They all looked to Jamie as the eldest. He screwed up his forehead, the effort of recollection a sore test. He spelt it out. 'Football-prohibited-by-order-of-the-council. Any- infraction-will be subject to a fine of fifty pounds.'

Isa nodded. 'The Cooncil, eh?'

'Aye, Isa,' the boys chimed. She threw her sons a warning look.

'*Mam*, we mean. Sorry, Mam,' they stuttered.

The pitch was situated at the bottom of the hill, part of the public park. It had been used by the town's boys for as long as she could remember, the grass maintained by the council, and there were two goalposts, one a bit squinty but useful.

'What about the posts?' she said.

'Away,' they howled.

'Good God. But how come there's gates? It's open ground.'

'Wire aw aroon the pitch and gates tied up wi chains.'

This was a problem, especially when you had seven sons. 'Right lads, nothing tae be done the noo, leave it wi me. Jist play in the street, and mind the windaes.'

What was the council up to? This was a local amenity. She'd go see Brendan Sweeney, the local councillor, knock on his door, whether he liked it or not. She surveyed the sky, stuck out her palm, the air was drying nicely. She'd hang those nappies out first.

With the nappies billowing on the line, and the crowd fed a stack of jam pieces, the older ones lining up to play penalties in the street, Isa lay Ben in the pram and stuck Charlie on the front seat, his feet soon kicking against her tummy as the pram sprung along the pavement.

Sweeney was a bampot. He'd been a union man till

he smelt the decay of the Yards and jumped on the Labour ticket. He wasn't to be trusted, partial to sweeteners and backhanders, but Isa needed to gauge for herself what was going on. Funny how there'd been no notice in the local paper or in the local gossip. She paced downhill to the pitch. It was a flat piece of ground on the periphery of the park, railings erected the full length and breadth of the field with nasty barbed wire strung on top. A set of padlocked metal gates sported a large white sign. She grabbed the cold steel chained around the lock and rattled the gates. Fifty pounds indeed.

She doubled back to Sweeney's house, parked the bairns at the gate, picked her way up the neglected path between banks of nettles, watching out for her nylons, and chapped.

Sweeney peeked around the door with a charmless smile. He smelled like the distillery.

'Oh, it's Mrs McMenamin.' He didn't look surprised. Word travelled fast.

'Brendan.' Isa looked down at his tiny feet.

He shifted back a spot. 'What can I do ye fer?' He chuckled at his wit.

'The fitbaw pitch?'

'Aye, The Council need the land.' He switched his eyes left, over her shoulder.

'Uh-huh.' Isa captured his gaze, brought it back centre.

'It's fer housing, we badly need housing.'

'Uh-huh.'

'Nothing tae be done. It's sorted.' He puffed out his tin man chest.

'Ah never heard of any notices.'

'It's on record.'

'Where?'

'Well, will be, Monday night, council meeting.'

The bastard squirmed from foot to foot now. He wasn't even a good liar.

'No decided then?'

'Well…'

'A bit premature, that.' Isa threw Sweeney her most withering look, one that Angus said shrank his goolies, turned, charged down the path, kicked off the brake and left the eejit to jangle.

Monday ran her ragged. Her nerves threatened to unstitch her, lay bare her anger and sense of injustice. The washing line snapped with the weight of nappies and she had to wash them again. Surely the council couldn't build on the pitch? The temptation was clear, flat land was at a premium, the town wedged between the Clyde and the hills. But also at a premium were football pitches for the weans.

The meeting was at seven thirty and when Angus came in at six she handed him her pinny which he held at arm's length in bemusement. She changed and left to his protests: 'It'll dae nae guid anyway.' Such was the apathy she'd met all along the street and through the neighbourhood. *Och, ye cannae change these things: better look tae yer back if yer crossin Sweeney.* But they signed her petition good naturedly enough even if they saw it as foolhardy.

The municipal building sat in colourful gardens, and was built from red sandstone, with Alexander Robb, the town's shipbuilding magnate, positioned centre-stage on a high plinth. Isa had only been there once, around the back where the blue lamp marked the police station, on that occasion to collect one very drunk Angus after a night out. She took a deep breath, smoothed down her summer dress and entered by the double doors into a reception area where a clerk stood behind a high desk.

'Ah'm here for the council meeting.' Her voice pinged off the walls.

The round faced, greasy haired clerk looked up, his eyes asquint. 'You're not Press, are you?'

'Do ah look like Press?'

'Ye never know these days.'

'Ah'm here as a member of the public.'

He waved towards another set of double doors. 'Sit in the back row. Don't interrupt proceedings.'

Isa tapped her lips with her forefinger and winked at him, gratified when he fell back on his swivel seat.

The chamber wasn't as grand as she'd expected, men in suits sitting around an old scratched table that might have been good in its time but was badly in need of a polish. Smoke hung between shiny bald pates and sulphurous pendant lights. The odour of dust, and old suits hung too long in fusty wardrobes, made her sneeze. She stifled a giggle, must be nerves, although funny enough she didn't feel nervous at all, now she was here. If an argy-bargy was called for she was up for it. She realised she'd giggled again when heads switched in her direction, only to turn away unimpressed. On the back row a young man, in checked shirt and slacks, stood, nodded and invited her to sit near him. He looked familiar and when he took up a notepad and pencil Isa remembered his photo in the Mail.

'McCann, Press,' he said, proffering a hand.

'McMenamin. Member of the Public,' Isa returned, smiling broadly.

'Touché,' he said. 'You have a special interest in tonight's proceedings?'

'Ah do.'

'Interesting.'

'Why?'

'First time I've had any company here.'

'Ye know the ropes then?'

'Sure: there's something you want to pitch to the council?'

Isa laughed. 'Aye, ye could say that.'

A gavel banged.

The meeting went on… and it went on, etcetera, etcetera, this application and that discussed, agreed, refused, mumbled over, dissected, dismissed. Then it came. Item 41. Planning application for privately built housing adjacent to the Municipal Park. Mumbles of *straightforward enough, unused land,* some shaking of heads, some patting of backs.

The greasy clerk asked, 'Any objections?'

Isa sprung up. 'Ah object,' she called out in her most authoritative voice, the one that got the boys in line.

What a bustle, what a furore, the newspaperman dropped his notebook and his pencil rolled away under the rows in front, the councillors' mutters reached a crescendo, Sweeney stood waving his arms in righteous indignation, on his mug an expression of… aye, it was disgusted disbelief, as though something had shit on him.

The clerk banged his gavel. 'Silence please. We must hear the lady.'

Isa looked sideways to McCann. He gesticulated her forward and she strode up to the table. Grunts, throat-clearing, bad tempers, fidgeting, red faces, messed up papers, stamping of boots. My, these were just grown boys, she knew about boys, no matter their age. They hated being cooped up, they wanted to get out of here, to the pub, or home to their wives to be pampered and told how special they were. Isa pinned each grumpy face in turn, until the sounds abated and they sat perfectly still, in order.

The chairman cleared his throat.

'On what grounds do you object, my dear lady, err, Miss, Mrs…?'

'Mrs McMenamin.'

'You have the floor.'

Isa raised herself up and began her prepared spiel: 'Ah object on the grounds that this land is for the amenity of the townspeople, gifted by the Robb family who founded the shipyards, and is appropriately used by the neighbourhood children as a football pitch which keep said children out of trouble, suitably exercised, biddable at home and school. The said site has been vandalised by the proposed building company whom ah'm sure have misused this good council's name by fencing it off and threatening children with fines if they trespass. Ah have here a petition signed by two hundred and twenty-four of my neighbours, your voters, protesting this development, and ah have here a lawyer's letter,' Isa waved her gas bill hoping no one would notice, 'proposing court action if said grounds are not returned forthwith to their former usage.'

Mouths hung open, one or two palms were pressed to chests, and the gavel hung aimlessly over the table.

Then came a stuttering whine. It was Sweeney. 'But, Mr Chairman, housing is badly needed. These will provide homes for…'

'Four bungalows for private sale.' The chairman said, his finger tracing a line on the open page in front of him.

'What?' said the councillor to his left.

'But it's just a piece of wasteland at the minute,' said Sweeney.

'Mrs McMenamin has just described how well it's used,' the chairman said.

Isa watched closely. Politics in action looked a lot like boys squabbling in the street.

There was jostling going on here, and there were allegiances that didn't seem to include Brendan Sweeney. He was in a wee gang of his own.

A vote was taken. Planning Permission Denied.

Isa stuffed her gas bill back in her pocket and glided around the table to proffer her thanks to the chairman. Oh, how they all hurriedly stood, each face glued to hers, eager for praise. What good boys they were. She didn't disappoint, gave each a warm smile. The newspaper man sat nonchalantly, feet on the back of a chair, pencil in his ear. He gave her the thumbs up. Sweeney hung back, a nasty grimace on his mug.

He'd have to be dealt with at some point. At some point after her appointment the next day, at some point after she'd kicked pregnancy number nine out of the park.

Katherine Davey

The Quarry

If you want to come up to the quarry at night – if you want to swim here, as the tradition is, under the full moon – don't worry about what they say: the ghost who stands on the path looking back as if waiting for someone to come down towards the wood. No. Nor the slates beyond the ridge thin as ice, likely to give beneath your foot, the blind-black tunnel through the rock, the water deep as the cliff face. Don't worry about all that.

They'll warn you of these things before long when you come to the village. Or you'll hear them spoken of at the post-office counter with the pleasure people speak of fear, or when you're waiting for your latte at Ria's on the Square, where they talk with hushed respect, even when Ria's away. What the quarry meant to the villagers before, when it was alive with men, and afterwards, in its quiet years of abandonment since before the first world war, you'll discover in the museum. There is a pair of headphones attached to the wall out of which speaks the last surviving quarryman. He'll be dead by now. Long dead. But he tells you still of the knell of the sledgehammers on the slopes and of the irascible foreman, deaf in one ear. There's no one here now who'd know how to draft the face edge of a stone, though there's a tea-shop called The Mason's Point, where even Ria – though her place is as much a café as it is a gallery – says they sell the best bara brith 'between the Poles'.

Ria stopped her run of quarry paintings about five years ago. But still she uses oblique references to it as her trademark. A flat wall of rock. A dark ring of water. She's made a good living. A better one than she was making when David and I moved here twelve years ago. Then she produced endless versions of the estuary, like every artist who comes here for the first time, like a self-portraitist never certain they've revealed quite what they intended. She'd been in the village for five months when we arrived. David had heard about it – that it was the place to go for creative entrepreneurs. He'd been put on Statins and read a book about a man in Chicago who packed up his life as an insurance broker and made chairs. So we sold the house in London and bought the cottage with the shed at the back, which David did up – a concrete floor, insulation, electricity – and he took up his old student hobby and began again to buy and restore furniture. Occasionally he'd get a commission for something new: a side table, or a lampstand or salad bowl, which he'd turn on the lathe.

In London I'd worked in an office where I rewrote medical reports for online journals. I liked the office. But mostly I liked to have to leave our flat, so as to go back to it and feel, daily, on unlocking the door onto our hallway, that little stab of joy in home.

I didn't need to work. When my father died (my mother had died ten years before, just after David and I got together), it was all left to me, the only child. But I wanted to work. So in our new cottage I set up in the room at the back beside the kitchen with my reference books, my laptop, a pot plant I'd had on my desk in Bloomsbury, and there I rewrote reports. They were case studies, mostly: 'Puerperal sepsis in rural Uganda', 'Therapeutic Hypothermia after Cardiac Arrest'. That kind of thing. Subjects no more remote to me in Wales than they'd been in London, yet somehow here I was aware of the willow leaves against the casement, of the quiet estuary beyond the street, the silent hills. The world seemed benign.

In the afternoons I checked David's website for furniture queries and then dug in the vegetable patch beside his workshop. Always, before the sun dipped behind the hills, he'd knock on the window and I'd look up from my gloved hands in the earth and see him holding a gouge or a fishtail chisel at his chin and tilting it up and down like a china cup. I'd nod and smile and he'd disappear in the reflections of the glass and come out a few minutes later with two mugs of tea.

Ria lived across the road from us. After her divorce she'd left Manchester, where she'd run a shop, she said, selling bits and bobs. Here she had a studio the width of her cottage that looked across a strip of field to the estuary footpath and the water beyond. When we met her she was selling canvases awash with greys and greens, distinguished by scratches of light or the red nick of a sail.

She first called round the day we moved in. Since then she turned up at least once a week, always bearing something, as if it were her front door key. It was a bag of onions the first time, still black with soil. The next, a baby bat. I loathed bats – not personally, but in the way some people loathe spiders. Spiders I liked. Bats made me shrink into myself. Ria laughed when I exclaimed at the little grey ball in her palm, but when she saw the real alarm in my face she apologised and took it out the back to David. The last time she came she brought a Tupperware of flapjacks, still warm from the oven. David crossed the garden from his workshop, smacking the sawdust from his jeans and, delicately, with dusty fingers, picked one from the box and put the whole in his mouth. He made a sound – pleasure, satisfaction – which for some reason made me see him as I had so often, above me in the dark.

Ria smiled. 'It's a new recipe – I'm glad it passes.'

'More than…' David managed.

'Will you stay for a drink?' I said. As I always did. As she always did.

In the living room Ria sank into the middle of the sofa. 'God, this heat!' she said. But her arms fell open, as if she invited the humid ache of it.

'Your studio must be pretty unbearable,' I said. I put a bowl of peanuts on the table beside her.

'Yeah. The last thing you'd expect in Wales.'

David came in and handed her a glass ticking with ice. She dipped towards him on the cushions, smiling as she always did – as if she were a very old friend of ours, one we hadn't seen for years. David had opened another bottle of tonic. By the middle of the week, I knew, I'd pour the flat remains of it down the sink. Then Ria would arrive at the door again, wielding some offering, I'd invite her in, and David would open another bottle, alive with fizz. He said the one-drink tins of tonic made him think of hotel bars. I should've bought them anyway, but I didn't, because I saw in them, not hotels, but a series of evenings of Ria. The bottle somehow held other possibilities – that David and I might find ourselves sitting down facing each other, perhaps, rather than both of us in our chairs facing her on the sofa; that we might spend an evening talking, as we used to. It wasn't that we didn't talk. We did. But that concentration, that bright focus I saw in him as she spoke, had rubbed away into something comfortable.

That night Ria wore a string top edged with glass beads that dragged the thin fabric into a vee between her breasts. Her shoulders were slender, hard and round, as if the bones had been smoothed off underneath, and her skin was perfect – a uniform, hairless gold, like something she'd gone off and bought, absolutely new.

'Hotter than '76,' David said. His socked feet were stretched out on the carpet. There was a curl of wood shaving clinging to one. 'I've got a great little fan — a Dyson.'

'Well I've resorted to painting entirely starkers.' Ria lifted her glass towards us and draped her arm along the sofa back. Her armpit was like the bowl of a shell. It was impossible its perfection was not apparent to David. It was impossible it didn't suggest to him the perfection of the other folds and crevices of her. 'Thank God no one on the estuary path ever looks *up* the hill.'

She laughed.

David and I laughed.

I thought of David going for his run along the estuary path every morning.

'All twitchers or joggers,' David said. 'Other things on their minds.'

'You'll stay for pasta, won't you?' I stood up. Why? Why did I invite what I dreaded? I think I thought it was a show of arms, not an invitation. A dare to fate. Do your worst, I'd rather take it all at once, than have you dish it out piecemeal.

So I went into the kitchen as I had every week and stared into the fridge, wondering over the etiquette of effort for the uninvited guest. From the living room came the low sound of David's voice and hers. I couldn't hear their words. But the pattern of their speech was becoming as familiar to me as that of the couple who'd lived on the other side of our thin-walled London flat. They used to talk at night, every night. And lying there, beside David, my head on his arm in the dark, or my book held beside his in the lamplight, I'd wonder whether they spoke like that ceaselessly, in every room of their flat.

'I went up to the quarry last night,' Ria said at the

kitchen table. 'It was heavenly – just me, the moonlight.'

'The quarry?' I said. 'The old slate quarry?'

David picked up the bottle of wine and held its mouth over her glass, the liquid already trembling at its tip. 'Top-up?'

She flicked him a smile of assent and returned her attention to me. The effect was disorientating, as if I were the guest. I saw myself for a moment being offered a top-up by a solicitous David, watching Ria get up and bring over to the table the remains of the Bolognese from the hob.

'Yes, on the other side of the estuary. But you've hardly been here long enough,' she said. She pulled up a bare knee, resting it against the table and gazed at us fondly. 'The first sight I had of you two – clambering out of your car, wheeling suitcases through the snow – you, Sarah, clutching an umbrella, David in his city-boy coat... *The* most unlikely sight.' She laughed, throwing her head back. Her knee fell outwards, her cotton skirt slipped down her thigh to pool beyond the table edge between her legs. I felt I was watching a masterful performance, in which the director had managed the exact slide of cloth and melt of light on her skin.

'Last summer I went up every week to swim,' Ria was saying. 'At night, usually. It's magical.'

'What, a river?' David said. 'Or a lake?'

'No *in* the quarry. They blocked up the tunnels – all except the highest one. In case of collapse or something – so it just filled up.' She lifted a shoulder. 'Rainfall I suppose. And ever since people've gone swimming there. It's a bit of a thing, though very cold. These tough Welsh.' She leant forward abruptly over the table. The kitchen light settled between her breasts. 'I'll take you – tomorrow night. A bottle of wine, the three of us, a midnight skinny dip.'

David grinned at her. 'Why not? While the heat lasts?'

She couldn't have expected the idea to appeal to me, as much as to David. 'Hm.' I said. 'Why not in daylight?'

Ria stretched her arms towards the ceiling, yawning. 'Oh no,' she dropped them back on the table. 'Moonlight's the tradition.'

So we went. David, Ria and I. What should I have done? If I'd an unremarkable way out, I'm not sure what it was.

David always got up before I did. He'd go for his run and by the time he got back, flushed with blood and salt air, I'd be making coffee. But the next morning, instead of stopping the alarm the moment it sounded and slipping from the bed, he rolled over and ran his hand about my waist, pulling me against him. 'David…' I mumbled into my pillow.

He began to kiss my neck and then moved downwards, down my spine, over my buttocks. Was this an apology? Because he knew I didn't want to go. Because he wanted to go enough despite that?

His mouth moved over my thigh. The stubble of his chin was at that in-between stage – not long enough, yet, to be soft, to be bearable for long between my legs. 'David…' He was dragging me downwards, rolling me over, and although I clutched at my pillow I was laughing, won over.

I didn't shower that day. I liked knowing that, that night, when I went with them up the valley I might catch the sharp scent of sex from my own skin as I walked up in the heat beside her.

We picked her up at ten. I had a backpack with my swimsuit, David's trunks, a couple of towels. David had his old cyclists' bag with the double strip of fluorescence that he'd used to take in to the city every day. In it was a bottle of wine, torches, three plastic wine glasses, peanuts and two slabs of chocolate. Ria was sitting on her garden wall. She had nothing with her but a headlamp, switched off, slung round her neck, and a bottle of cava balanced on her bare thigh. She looked young in the moonlight – a girl in shorts and a vest. Innocent. I felt a spring of affection, and then she slid off the wall, smiling, holding the bottle out before her for balance, and she was again familiar to me.

'You two! Over-prepared as ever,' she said. 'You got a tent?'

It was a twenty-minute drive. From the car park we could see the miners' track running up the side of the valley. It vanished in the wood and emerged again, winding upwards. The night was clear and under the full moon the valley was bathed in light. On the ridge of the hill, against the violet sky, was the black arm of the winch beside the buffer stop of the mine's old narrow-gauge rails.

'You'll need your torches in the wood.' Ria knocked the car door shut with her hip. 'You did bring them?'

'Yup.' David took the bottle from her hands and shoved it into his backpack.

The heat of the day was still trapped in the earth as we began to walk up. Our legs were chalk-white in the moonlight, the patch of sweat in the small of David's back dark as noon shadow. We'd been going for about half an hour when David put a hand on my neck and

ran his thumb back and forth. A discreet encourage-
ment. He knew, had it been just him and me, that I'd
have stopped to catch my breath — briefly, but at least
once. I didn't want his knowing, less so his telling me
that he knew I'd not stop, exactly because I was not —
as Ria was — spry as a whippet. I stepped widely on the
track past a spray of bramble, leaving his hand to fall
away.

We stopped when we entered the wood, suddenly
blind beyond the moonlight. David took off his
backpack. My eyes began to habituate. I saw the dense
shapes of the ferns, the pines, alder and ash. The trees
were still, the warm air motionless between their leaves.
David handed me a torch. Behind me Ria adjusted the
headlamp about her forehead and switched it on. A
strip of path and the bristly trunk of a pine leapt into
detail; the rest blinked into darkness.

'Go on,' Ria said. 'I'll follow.'

So I walked on, David behind me, my torch sweep-
ing the ground, catching the elbow of a root, the jut of
stone from the ground.

'Ow!'

'Ria?' David's beam looped back over the trees to
the path behind us. 'Ria?'

'Nothing! Pine needle in my sock… Go on!'

I turned to walk on. But David waited. And having
made my step forward I was unable to change my mind.
Had I feared nothing between them I'd have stopped.
So I kept on, slowly. My boot made little sound on the
loamy earth. It was as if I were tiptoeing, as if I were
pretending I wasn't there at all. I heard Ria's laugh
someway behind me, then silence again, except for my
muffled steps.

I stopped when I came out the other side of the
wood and switched off my torch. For a moment all was

again black until my eyes adjusted and the path emerged between the bracken, pale as flour. It broadened to a shelf of rock and then climbed steeply for thirty yards or so until it doubled back on itself below the ridge. I looked back into the wood, watching for the glimmer of David's light. My legs were humming with heat, my T-shirt damp.

There was a flicker between the trees, then the full glare of a torch and another, smaller light held higher, bobbing, it seemed, beside David's wavering beam. Ria's voice. Then David's laughter. Then a sound like a scuffle and David's torch vanished.

'David?'

'Sarah!' Ria called back. 'I'm an idiot!' Their torches emerged blindingly from the darkness. I closed my eyes, waiting for the scarlet shifting of the light over my eyelids to go.

'I couldn't undo my lace,' she said. 'So having yanked my trainer off, I couldn't get it back on.'

She had an arm over David's shoulders. With her lopsided stretch, her vest had ridden up above the band of her shorts. David's hand about her lay flat over the ridge of denim and the bare skin of her waist. She was holding one trainer in her hand, her foot in a short sock suspended in the air beside her calf. 'Your sweet husband has been my crutch.' She hopped away from him on one foot and sat down on the side of the path. 'I hope you don't mind.'

'Of course not,' I said. 'David's always been good in a crisis.'

I heard myself, the edge in my voice, with dismay. I'd determined to give them nothing. To be careless, bright, untirable. I dropped to my haunches beside her. 'My nails might help.'

'Please, yes. Could – oh! Got it.' She tugged the

lace free and pulled at the tongue of her trainer to slip her foot inside.

I stood up again. David slung his bag off and took out his water bottle. He offered it to me. 'For an experienced mountaineer…' He smiled at me, but his words were for her, like a nudge in the softness below her ribs. I felt again some intimacy between them. Some understanding that'd sprung up while I arranged peanuts in bowls in the kitchen, or opened tins of tomatoes and chopped garlic. Or had he seen her in her studio one day on his run and stood, gazing, over the wall?

Ria was on her feet again. 'Right,' she said, slapping the dirt from her shorts.

I imagined her, paintbrush in hand as he walked up to the open doors, wearing – what? I saw him step inside, breathing hard, sweaty, the early mist of the estuary in his hair. *I've resorted to painting entirely starkers.* Birdwatchers and joggers, he'd said. *Other things on their minds.*

'There's the tunnel,' Ria said.

We'd come up on top. What had seemed a narrow ridge from the path below was in fact the edge of the broad spine of the hill, across which was strewn stack upon stack of discarded slate. There was no vegetation here at all. On the far side was a flat-faced bulk of rock, as if a god had forced into the humped back of the hill an Olympian cleaver and pared away its flank. At the foot of this grey-lit hulk of rock was a black hole.

'How do we reach it?' I asked.

'We follow the tramway,' Ria said. 'David, could you come here?'

David had stopped, now he turned to her, but she put a hand to his shoulder, shifting him round, and unzipped his backpack. She took out the water bottle and raised it, tipping it carelessly, so that the water ran down the curve of her throat.

She wiped her mouth with her wrist, her other hand resting on David's opened backpack, and waved the bottle further along the ridge, where the winch stood, its black arm raised. 'That's the start of it.'

The tramway was narrow. The rails themselves were partly obscured by broken slates and the gradual inching of the land over a near-century. It's not the narrowness of the ridge, but the slates that can be dangerous – they give easily. When we reached the low mouth of the tunnel and David switched on his torch, the tracks gleamed clear and blackly wet ahead of us.

'Who were these people,' David said. 'Hobbits?'

'Used to stooping, I expect,' I said.

He bent and scanned the tunnel roof. From inside came the faint drip of water. 'It's pretty dank in there. Where's this swimming pool of yours?'

'Just the other side.' Ria adjusted her headlamp. 'So, keep your head low and a hand up. Like this.' She dipped her head and raised one hand to her forehead, palm outwards, like a child pretending to be an elephant. She stood up again, looking into David's face, which I couldn't see, and burst out laughing. 'I'm serious, David – it's craggy. You'll split your head open.'

I tried to picture her – a woman who couldn't undo her shoelaces – alone, up here, at night. Or perhaps she'd no more come up here alone at night than she'd been unable to undo her laces? Had they slept together? Was that that look of vigour he came home with after his morning run? Did she want me to think it? Or did she mean, simply, to flaunt herself before him, to see in his eyes and mine what power she had?

'When you come out of the tunnel there's a narrow ledge – that's all – about six feet above the water. So don't walk straight on unless you want wet clothes,' Ria was saying. 'You can use the ladder from the ledge or jump – or dive, which is what I do – as deeply as you like. If the water were drained off you'd be on the cliff face so there's nothing to knock into. You know Mr Robinson?'

'The ironmonger,' I said.

'Yeah, Mark. His father started it. He used to bring Mark up on Sundays in the summer. Mark doesn't come anymore.' She laughed. 'He says he prefers to watch the rugby.'

'He doesn't know what he's missing,' David said.

Except he did know, didn't he? He used to come every Sunday. David must be thinking of now, of Ria. We were going to go out onto that ledge. We were going to strip – she was, certainly – her body blue in the moonlight. She'd dive into the water – not jump in panicked determination, or creep down the ladder, dreading the chill on her warm skin.

When David and I were first together we got drunk one night in a little pub below London Bridge. We'd been talking about something. I can't remember what. But we got onto desire. And he'd said – leaning in and gazing at me – that he hadn't a clue what became of desire in the end, but love me he would for the rest of his life. Then, desire had seemed nothing to me. A given. Mutually insatiable. It was love I wanted. So his words were then, and for years after, like a bar of gold I banked in my heart.

'Right, David, you go first,' Ria said. 'I'll make sure Sarah's all right behind.'

'I'm fine. No pine needles, my laces are done up.'

David walked past me, his hand sliding over the

hollow of my back. 'Watch your head, love.'

He bent, looking into the dark. I put out a hand and touched him. Not in affection, particularly. Perhaps I wanted my hand, at least, to grasp something familiar. My fingers fell at the base of his curved spine as he ducked and walked into the tunnel.

I hitched my bag on my shoulder and followed. My torch beam crossed his ahead of me and gleamed over the rock. My foot slid. I toppled, regained my balance and reached out, trying to find the rock wall. Then I remembered the jagged tunnel roof and put my palm to my forehead.

Ria's headlamp behind me had vanished. I could no longer see David ahead. 'Slow down!'

'What?' His voice reached me, a little muffled by the angles of rock. His torch reappeared – brilliantly, directly in my eyes. The light caught the line of his jaw, the contours of his face, the flare of his nostrils. 'Where's Ria?'

Water dripped onto my neck. 'Just behind me.'

We stood in silence. David's trainer rasped over the wet grit of the passage. No light came from behind.

'Ria?' I called back, my voice light.

No answer.

David lifted his head. *'Ria!'*

'Perhaps her laces are giving her trouble.'

I didn't see if he smiled – his torch had shifted to the space behind me.

And then a beam danced over the rock and Ria's footsteps sounded and she appeared, grinning beneath her headlamp. 'Bats! A whole colony – come and see!'

'You're joking?' I said.

'God! – sorry – of course…'

David stood where he was.

'Go and see,' I said to him. *Go on*, I thought. *Don't*

think I'll compete with her for you.

'Ok.'

'Don't jump in without us,' Ria said, 'or you'll be out before we're back – it's too cold to stand for long.'

When you come out of that tunnel at night, under a full moon and a clear sky you'll see why it's worth it. Around you the massive slopes of the quarry rise up like the sides of a bowl, so that standing at the tunnel mouth you have to tilt your head back to see the disc of starry sky above. Before you the water lies like silver. Its temperature averages twelve degrees in June. By the end of August, after a long summer, it can reach fifteen. But rarely more: the quarry walls admit the sun for only an hour a day.

I was sweating with heat and anger. I sat down to undo my boots, pulled them off, my socks after them, shoving them into the boots. The skin of my bare feet, ridged and hot and damp from my socks, glowed blue-white. I stood up, stripped off my T-shirt, bra, shorts, knickers and bundled them beside my boots. The rock beneath my soles was warm from the day. If she was going to wear nothing I would not cover myself. Why should I, before my own husband? I would not play the neighbour while she played the wife. And I would not wait for them, as she recommended, with her condescending fondness – as if I hadn't the stamina she had, hadn't the sense she had – while she and David fumbled through the hot darkness. No. I'd not be here when they came back – the timid Sarah, afraid of bats, afraid of the cold, afraid of the dark water, afraid of being left...

My feet gripped at the stone edge, my toes curved towards the water. My feet felt tender on the rock. I shifted my toes, raised my hands, and jumped.

The water was like a fist against my ribcage and then the burning cold followed the blow, as if my skin were stripped from me as I sank. I kicked once, twice, upwards and burst out into the night air, gasping, wanting to cry out in fright. My head spun at the shock of it, my chest cringing. I kicked and kicked, gasping until the dizziness went and my breath steadied. Gradually, as I kicked and gasped, the fierce chill softened and a thrill bloomed through me. I looked back to the rock ledge, forgetting my anger, wanting, simply, to see David see me in this moment. But the mouth of the tunnel was empty. I could see only the pale bundle of my clothes on the ledge.

I turned and struck out for the far side of the pool. Here the rock overhangs a little, so when the moon is high it seems to loom in shadow, while flanking it the rock face is crisp with light. I reached it – my body quick and cold with life – and turned, treading water, looking back, upwards, along the reach of rock above me to the sky. Here, if you rest your head against the rock wall as you tread water the rock seems steady at first, then it begins to fall. The Falling Face, the people call it who come here. A blackness that seems perpetually to be tumbling towards you and its dark self in the water. If you keep looking you feel yourself falling too, forwards, downwards, as if the water were becoming insubstantial, like air, and you felt below your kicking feet the rock plummeting away in great, petrified silence towards the valley floor.

My heart lurched, and I pushed off in sudden fright from the shadowed rock towards the bright centre of the pool. There I stopped and trod water, the cold still sweet against me.

'Wonderful!' I shouted upwards. '...*derful...erful... ful.*' My voice echoed over the bowl of the quarry and then sank into silence.

I lay back, floating. My body gleamed white, my nipples puckered and dark.

Where were they?

I twisted upright and looked again towards the tunnel mouth, the little ledge of rock before it.

'*David?…vid?…vid?*' The word gathered and fell still over the surface of the water.

My bundle of clothes seemed to have grown luminous on the ledge, as if the moon were still gaining brightness. The water – as Ria said – is not bearable for long. I'd begun to shiver. Five minutes is long enough. If you do come here, make sure you bring a thick jumper for when you get out.

What were they doing? Surely David, wouldn't, couldn't, be touching her in the dark beneath the bats?

'*Ria!…ah…ah…*' And then again, silence.

My anger returned. Just like that. Swift as the cold. I kicked back towards the ledge. I'd get out, I'd walk back, past them, wherever they were, whatever they were doing – groaning in the dark between the rails in the wet of the tunnel, pressed against its dripping walls. I reached the ledge and looked for the ladder. The rock was blank above me. I looked along its length, to the left, to the right. I could see nothing but the ridges of hacked slate. I blinked, scanning the shadows carefully, thinking its iron rails must be too dark to show, too rusted to catch the light. Nothing. I kicked back towards the centre of the pool. Perhaps I was too close to see it. I swept the ledge with my eyes: and above it, its edge, its left flank, its right. Then I began to turn, slowly, kicking at the black water below me, my eyes scanning every face – though for what, or whom, a ladder would have been screwed into the cliff out of reach of the tunnel, I did not think. Ria had swum here last year, every week… just two nights ago…

I struck back to the ledge. My fingers felt slow. The cold was seeping into me. I began to swim along beside the rock, running my hand over it, searching it for metal. Nothing. Nothing. My fingers pried half-numbly between the ridges and angles, as if the rungs of a ladder might hide, small and discreet, like a gem to be discovered. And then, on the very right of the wall below the tunnel, just above the waterline, my hand caught the sharp projection of metal. A bolt. I looked up above it and there, six feet above me, at the ledge, was another, and attached to it a little scab of metal – a broken rung.

'David! …vid…vid…vid!' I shouted.

Ria had swum. She'd got out. She said she'd swum. She said… No. She said she'd been here… Had she swum? She'd implied… But they would not leave this, they would not – the people who looked after the paths, who were clearing the pines to encourage native trees, who'd put up the sign at the bottom of the track, 'Old Quarry Road'…

'David! …vid…vid…vid!' My voice rolled about the rock faces above me. 'Ria…ah…ah…ah!'

'David, there's no ladder…der…der…er…er!' The echoes bounced back and forth, they seemed at first louder than my own voice, and then they ran together, like a distant party of people passing by above me and moving off down the hill.

David. My head felt light with panic. David. I put my hand to the bolt, gripping it between a finger and thumb to anchor myself beside the rock, kicking my legs slowly beneath me. My feet began to feel heavy and dumb – as if I were wearing my boots.

'Help me!…me…e…e!'

I was treading water out of sync, one leg slower,

flailing to the side. I felt a dull thud. I'd knocked my knee on the rock wall before me. It was not painful. I stayed where I was, kicking, holding the bolt. But the cold began to subdue me. My breath grew thin and tired. I worked back towards the centre of the pool, just to move, to lift my arms against the icy water, to help the blood quicken. I turned onto my back, half floating, half pushing with my hands and feet. I felt clumsy, my timing was out. My hands failed to cup the surface, my feet slipped sideways, not bearing me up, not working together. I saw then that my knee was leaking blood and fear shot through me like a new, inner coldness.

In that temperature you can last two hours. You should last one. But there are other factors. Body fat. Height. State of mind. Above all, a means of keeping afloat. It's not hypothermia that kills most people. It's drowning from cold incapacitation. You become exhausted. Your blood vessels close up, to shore up your warmth about your heart, but because of that your muscles and nerves stop responding. Your limbs stop functioning. Your fingers stiffen and splay, sliding meaninglessly through the water. You can't grip. You could lift your fingers again, for instance, to that single bolt in the slate wall, but this time you'd find your hand was dull as a lump of meat. And so – and it doesn't take very long, sometimes only fifteen minutes if you're slight – you sink.

'David …id…id….'

If you come up here on an overcast night the quality of the echo is not the same as on a clear night. It's more contained, as if you were in sports hall. And if you come up in the day the place seems quite different. Smaller. More domestic. The sort of place you'd bring children. The ladder bolts had rusted to such a degree over the winter that the ladder was considered a hazard and taken down in the spring. They intended to have another one fixed up. But they hadn't, yet. So in the meantime they'd nailed a barrier with a notice across the tunnel entrance. DANGER. DO NOT SWIM. DEEP WATER. NO MEANS OF EXIT.

The people who come here now sit on the ledge as they pull off their boots and talk about it. They take photos.

The night we came the barrier was gone. Someone had taken it away. They never did discover who, or why. It was found two days later on the valley side. Ria had seen no sign of it the night she'd come up alone. But she'd not swum, just sat on the ledge – so the newspapers reported – sketching the quarry in the moonlight. A preparatory drawing, which they printed in the papers alongside the reports. She completed the painting itself in the weeks that followed, and that they printed some months later, with a follow-up on the measures taken since the tragedy. That's what they called it. David, the newspapers said, was too stunned with grief and shame to say anything at all. Anything except that he'd not known, he'd had no idea that they'd been gone so long, that they'd spent so long away from me. Twenty-five minutes. That was all. He said it'd felt to him like ten.

Einstein said that, didn't he? Put your hand on a hot stove for a minute and it seems like an hour. Sit beside a pretty girl for an hour and it seems like a minute. Well, it was twenty-five minutes in our case. To him it seemed like ten. To me ... well, it's been endless.

I remembered in that time, as I grew colder and my kicking weaker and my head so heavy that I lay back as I had at the start and floated, looking up at the stars – I remembered what David and I had been talking about that night at London Bridge. The paradox of desire. Whether it was possible to want something you already had.

If you come up here now to swim you'll find a new ladder bolted with steel where the old one was. And they've cut a second way out: a series of steps in the rock ledge. So if you like you can walk down into the water and back up out of it, as you might a swimming pool.

And you needn't worry about me. I avoid the pool at night and I rarely go further than the bend in the path above the wood. I see David, often. He comes up alone when the moon is full, or near full, and haunts the rock ledge above the water. On those nights I can bear the pool. I stand beside him and look at him while he stares at the water, and I tell him about the woman in Cardiff who'd rung that morning to order two dozen salad bowls for her shop, and I tell him I'd have liked a child, and that I like his new cottage, which I can see from the ridge. And I ask him questions that of course he cannot answer. Sometimes, when I'm feeling brave, I stand directly before him and look into his eyes and tell him he need not come back. That he must not. But he gazes through me at the water. So I walk back beside him down the path until we reach the entrance to the woods, where I stop. There I stand and watch until he vanishes in the darkness.

Raphael Falco

The Day John Lennon Died

The day John Lennon died I had worked four sixteeners in a row. By December, Hiep and I were working alone in the kitchen, no prep cooks or sous-chefs, sixteen hours a day, seven days a week. Hiep said we only needed a dishwasher to help with the lifting, fetching, and cleaning. This crazy schedule started in July, about a month after we took over the kitchen from the original chef. Edward, the manager, didn't approve, but the owners were okay with it.

I resisted the kitchen coup at first, until the owners appealed to my vanity and Hiep promised to lead my footsteps from behind. So I fired every cook and dishwasher, including the high-carat culinary-school chef. Edward objected to that too. But when Hiep and I agreed to take only half the cooks' total salaries, even he saw the logic. They made me chef, which was a travesty with Hiep in the kitchen. For my debut act, at Hiep's command, I refused all meat, fish, and produce, sending it straight back to the purveyors without even opening the cartons. When the phone started ringing I told them one by one they should be flying the Jolly Roger the way they'd been robbing the place. The other chef had been a coke-addled cretin but even he didn't deserve the decomposing trash those purveyors passed off on him. They got their comeuppance, though, when they saw Hiep standing like a white-coated guardian of the Buddhist hell at our delivery entrance, waving away van after van.

I knew Hiep only as the Chinaman when he started because that was what they called him in the kitchen. He arrived with two other workers from the temp-agency, a Dominican grill man and a surly black dishwasher. The grill man was tall for a Dominican and he carried his own set of knives wrapped in a yellow dishrag. You could tell he'd spent a lot of time in kitchens by the way he came in that first night, swaggering a bit and smiling all around.

"You the chef?" he said cheerfully to the rangy cook wearing a red bandana on his head.

The chef nodded imperceptibly. He was working the sauté, dropping in pinches of rosemary like propitiations.

"You got some mess here," the Dominican observed with a sweep of his hand. "What you want me to do?"

"Make salads. Can you make a Niçoise?"

"Sure, no problem. But I'm a grill man."

"Just do what I say."

"Sure, sure. You the boss."

Meanwhile the Chinaman stood silently at the doorway. He was short and barrel-chested and had a long scar on his forehead that was shaped like one of those baling hooks the longshoremen carried in *On the Waterfront*. He looked about forty-five, and I felt a pang of regret that an old man like him still had to go out on temp-cook jobs. But it was only a pang. I had my own job to concentrate on and the mayhem in the kitchen that night had everybody on edge. With the addition of the Dominican and the Chinamen we now had five cooks in cramped quarters, only we weren't working like five spokes in the same wheel. The chef wasn't overseeing our work at all. Dupes from the waiters got slotted onto the rack in normal chronological order and the chef, bless his skipping heart, was actually working on every dupe in chronological order, one-by-one as they came in. It was daylight madness. Instead of making, say, two racks of lamb, three pastas primavera, and a couple of sole almandines at once, and putting out a few tables in quick succession, the chef was pampering each order on its own. No one, least of all the chef, was working as an expediter. The other cooks read the dupes and organized them on their own initiative. Stations were jumping ahead and leapfrogging each other, a server's worst nightmare. The food from the grill kept coming up ahead of the food from the sauté and was left to dry out under the heat lamps. The salads wilted or weren't ready on time. The Dominican was right: it was a mess, like watching a great empire collapse because the ruler couldn't keep his satraps in line.

The chef was so busy at the sauté, knapping a serving of seared shrimp in his patented rosemary cream sauce, he didn't seem to see the breakdown in the stations or even notice the Chinaman in the doorway. So the Chinaman waited, his arms dangling at his sides, his powerful, pudgy hands sticking out of a borrowed chef's jacket. They'd given him a jacket to fit his shoulders, but the sleeves were much too long. He rolled back the cuffs, but they were still too long.

Excruciating minutes ticked by, each one a decade in kitchen time. We waited. At last the chef finished his *crevettes trufflés* with polenta—an odd propinquity on the plate, for sure, but his whole menu read like a forced march of NATO countries. He was about to move on to another dish headed for the same table when he spotted the Chinaman.

"What the hell are you doing?" he snapped. Then he recovered himself and tried to remember what they'd taught him in culinary school about dealing with the foreign help. He raised his voice. "Can you speak English? Do you understand me?"

The Chinaman ducked his head to say yes.

"Good. Great. Shrimp? You know shrimp?"

Another duck of the head.

"Good. All right, we need more shrimp. You know how?" The chef ordered a dishwasher to bring over the plastic tub of frozen shrimp that were soaking in water. The dishwasher drained the shrimp with his hand and dropped the tub on the center worktable. "You know how cut?" The chef said, lapsing into Pidgin English for better clarity. "You know clean?"

The Chinaman gave no indication if he understood. As an answer he merely pulled the round plastic tub toward him. The chef said, "Over there, over there," and waved the Chinaman to the stainless steel prep table along the wall. The Chinaman slid the tub off the table and hefted it across to the prep table without the least change of expression. He must have known cleaning shrimp was a prep man's or dishwasher's job, degrading for a cook of any standing. You can bet the Dominican wouldn't have been happy about cleaning thirty pounds of frozen shrimp. But the Chinaman never flinched. He turned his back to us and started on the tub.

I stopped thinking about him for the next few minutes. My job was to work the pasta strainers, though by the time the temp-cooks arrived I'd given up any hope of doing the job right. Only a mind reader could have followed the chef. There was no way to tell when he would complete a table and call for the pasta, which had to be the last dish. No pasta could survive the heat lamps. I found myself boiling and draining, waiting, then giving the different pastas a flash re-dip in the boiling pot. Then, more times than not, I surreptitiously dumped it in the garbage before it became a plate of glue. The waste broke my heart. But there was no other way while the chef dawdled over his fey creations.

After another age, the chef finished the second plate for the same table that was getting the *crevettes trufflés*. He straightened up, beaming around the kitchen with glazed triumph and surveying his minions. We were all pretending to be too busy to stop and beam back. Except the Chinaman. He was standing just as he'd been standing a few minutes before, facing the chef, arms dangling. There was nothing defiant about his posture, he wasn't even smiling. But he also wasn't pretending to work. He just stood there at mild attention with his back to the prep table.

This was too much for the chef. He forgot his culinary school manners and started bellowing at the Chinaman.

"What do you think you're doing?! What the *fuck* are you doing!! I told you to do those shrimp! We need shrimp, you lazy—" he stopped himself, but slammed down a pan he was holding and started toward the Chinaman. "I don't know where they get you people from, why do they send me such fuckin'…such fuckin'…"

We had all stopped what we were doing by now and were staring at the chef. He was a tall, big-boned guy, and pretty menacing when he moved fast.

But the Chinamen didn't budge. He just kind of cocked his head and watched the chef like a museum visitor at a diorama.

"You get out of my kitchen, you lazy fuck! Out! Out of here before I throw you the fuck out! *Do you hear me?!!*" He was shouting now, and he grabbed the front of the Chinaman's white jacket. "Maybe this is how they work in China, but you're not in fucking China now, you lazy—"

He didn't get any further than that. The Chinaman locked the chef's hand against his own chest with one of those powerful pudgy hands, snapped the hand down, and broke the hold. He shoved the chef backward, not so gently.

"Not Chinese, *Vietnamese!*" he said. Then he threw the plastic tub on the floor: "Shrimp all done."

"That's impossible—!" the chef said. "You—"

Everybody stared at the Chinaman.

It *was* impossible, as the chef said. Nobody could clean and butterfly thirty pounds of shrimp in ten minutes. It was impossible, but there it was. When the Chinaman moved the plastic tub we all saw three neat stacks of perfectly cleaned shrimp on the stainless steel prep table.

"That's impossible," the chef murmured again. He stood to his full height, suddenly officious, and made a pretense of examining the shrimp.

"Not Chinese, Vietnamese," the Chinaman said. "I go now." He started unbuttoning his chef's jacket.

"No, wait. Wait," the chef said.

"I go now."

The Chinaman didn't go. He ended up staying, and staying a long time, which changed my life. I didn't know it was going to change my life when I clocked out after that miracle-of-the-shrimp shift, but I remember the night. I remember standing outside on the sidewalk for a moment. The entrance was crowded with men trying to get into the restaurant, and the bouncers had set up a velvet rope near the door. I stepped around the rope and pushed my way to the curb where I looked back at the sign. *Wilde,* it said in blue neon script, with the *e* blinking on and off every few seconds. The blinking was deliberate. *Wilde* was the pioneer gay restaurant on the Upper West Side. The owners knew all about Oscar Wilde and the name *Wilde* was supposed to remind everyone of the injustice done to a brilliant writer because of his sexual leanings. The Stonewall rebellion against the New York City cops was still fresh in people's minds and the politics of naming a restaurant *Wilde* was inspired advertising.

The name contained an impish double-entendre, also inspired advertising. This was 1980 and the Baths were still open downtown. Gay pride had grown wings and all our customers were flying, flying, flying. Edward and the owners liked to think of themselves as part of the scene, fellow-travelers, and they insisted we keep the kitchen open until 3 AM as part of the fun. Things got very wild after midnight. Men in all states, destroyed-by-madness, starving-hysterical-naked, found their way to the kitchen, demanding heavenly manna or golden nectar and inviting me to join them on a trip to Shangri-La.

*

The Chinaman wasn't a Chinaman at all, of course, as he kept telling us. He was Vietnamese and in those early weeks he was just a squat Asian enigma working the prep table. He never spoke—though we all heard the soundless thunder of his knifework. Even the addled chef seemed to sense an aura of untouchable superiority. We kept trying to talk to him, but nobody got much more than a grunted word. Then it came to me, a quiet revelation. A Vietnamese man of his age, I figured, a chef, would have been forced to speak French in colonial Vietnam. Now, by 1980, I'd already lived in France for a while—but that's not part of this story—so one afternoon, almost as a lark, I said a few sentences in French. There was a moment of hesitation on his part, and then the dam broke once and for all. Our Chinaman-who-wasn't started talking that minute and never stopped as long as we worked together. He could only talk to me, nobody else knew French, which was a bit of secret serendipity. The French was difficult to understand, sometimes a kind of tri-lingual creole, but the gist was clear. His name was Hiep, he had been the master chef at a luxury hotel in Saigon, with seven chefs and innumerable sous-chefs working under him. When Saigon fell, the Viet Cong put him in a prison camp for being an imperialist lackey. But he escaped from the camp and got to New York, I never found out how. He had been bombed, captured, and tormented, and he had a small metal plate in his head which made him a bit crazy when the kitchen got too hot.

Hiep had watched every move of every so-called chef from the day he'd arrived from the temp-agency. After the dam busted, in an uninterruptible diatribe, he itemized the faults and flaws and unforgivable crimes he'd witnessed from his corner of the kitchen. Nothing had escaped his eye. He laughed at the way the chef handled the sauté, the way the grill man dawdled, and the waste and delay among the prep cooks. He shook his head, appalled—but also puzzled—by the chef's blind naiveté with purveyors. Station by station, he levelled a comprehensive, withering critique of each cook in turn, night after night, all from memory. I shuddered as he got around to me, but he spared me the hammer. He liked two things about me, he said. I didn't work like an American and I had "cook's hands"—*mains de cuisine*—because I was the only one among all the "chefs" who didn't sauté every dish on the highest flame. Faint praise, maybe, but enough to tantalize me back then.

*

The day John Lennon died we were so busy I didn't even realize what had happened until nearly midnight.

Indications filtered through a little earlier, like subliminal suggestions, but I didn't put them together until afterwards. The dishwasher was playing the kitchen radio full blast and, as I dipped and turned from the stove to the serving table, I noticed with a tickle of pleasure that they were playing one Beatles song after another. At one point two of the waiters did a campy Broadway rendition of "Imagine" while they were waiting for their food. But the nickel didn't drop until I heard swells and falls of "Give Peace a Chance" coming from the dining room like Pentecostal choruses.

Hiep and I exchanged looks. I don't think the song meant much to him but we were both puzzled by the singing. I shifted the pans off the burners and we walked out through the swing doors. The dining room was quite a sight. The men sitting on the banquettes had their arms over each other's shoulders and were swaying in rhythm as they howled, "*All we are sayyyinnnggg, is give peace a chance.*" Some of the stoned-out ones were dancing like college girls up on the tables. The waiters were clapping, the bartenders were pouring faster than ever, even the busboys had stopped clearing and stood singing with their arms loaded down with dirty plates—and underneath it all, like background music from the wrong soundtrack, an irritating disco beat thrummed and rumbled from the overhead speakers.

But the scene was tilted, everything seemed wrong to me. I pulled a waiter close and asked in his ear, "What's going on?"

"Are you kidding?" he yelled back. "Where have you been?"

"Just tell me!" I shouted.

"They shot John Lennon! You gotta get out more, Maro!" Then he laughed and jiggled away to join three or four customers who had formed a chorus line and started kicking in time to "Give Peace a Chance."

"Who? Who shot him?" I shouted across at him.

"Over at the Dakota," he said.

I turned to Hiep and tried to explain what had happened, what was going on. But it was pointless, he couldn't grasp it. He shrugged and disappeared back into the kitchen.

I stood on the threshold between the kitchen and that raucous dining room scene. Through the clear panel on the swing door I saw Hiep ease the pans back onto the burners. He unfolded his horn-rims and bent close to read the two dupes we'd been working on. I let him finish the orders.

A waiter sliced through the tables heading for the kitchen. I stopped him at the door.

"Where are you going?" I asked.

"Ordering," he said.

"No," I said. "The kitchen's closed."

"What?" He tried to push past me. "You can't close the kitchen now. It's early, it's not even 11 o'clock. I have an order—"

"It's 11:45. I told you, the kitchen's closed."

The waiter stepped back. He was suddenly furious. "What the fuck?" he said. "You can't close the kitchen now. Look at this place. I'm *ordering*!"

"You heard me."

"Does Edward know? I'm going to tell Edward."

"Go ahead," I said.

I knew there would be trouble now but the decision was the decision. The kitchen would close early. It seemed like the least I could do, the least gesture.

"Hiep!" I called through the swing door, without actually leaving the threshold to the dining room.

"Hiep, the kitchen's closed. C'est fermée la cuisine."

"Fermée? Porquoi fermée? Quelles heures sont-ils maintenent?"

"N'importe pas. La cuisine est fermée. D'accord?"

Hiep stared at me. I could see the jagged contempt in his movements as he shoved his glasses into his pocket and turned off the burners. He was shaking his head the way he always shook it at Americans.

By that time Edward had stormed across from the bar. He was red in the face, hysterical and uncoordinated, flapping his arms. I pushed past him and elbowed my way out through the bar to the front door. My mind was blurred by impulsiveness, my imagination running away. The line of men inside the velvet ropes seemed to be a single live organism, a gorged boa twisting slowly in its throes. I wondered if anybody noticed me, if I looked different to them.

It didn't matter if they noticed me. I could imagine exactly what they saw, a cook in kitchen whites staring east at the Hayden Planetarium. Not a rare sight, a cook on the sidewalk getting some evening air, not in those restaurant days on the Upper West Side. The cook lit a cigarette, also not surprising. He crossed the street and stood on the far curb watching the blinking light in the *Wilde* sign. He knew what the men waiting in line didn't know. He knew the kitchen was closed. The cook turned his back, a gesture, and stared again at the dome of the Planetarium. He stared and smoked unmoving until he realized Hiep had changed his clothes and was standing beside him. Hiep laid his hand on the cook's shoulder and murmured something in French. The cook felt Hiep's touch shiver electrically through his nerves. But he didn't reply. He didn't reply because, just at that moment, staring blankly at the dome, he saw that nothing would protect vanity from dull truth.

Gerard McKeown

A History of Fire

Spontaneous combustion runs in the males of my family. My granda, my dad, and my uncle all died of it. All of them were heavy drinkers, with heavy bodies and fiery tempers. People have asked if I'm worried it will happen to me. I'm hopeful it will skip a generation. As crazy as spontaneous combustion sounds, it wouldn't be the worst way to die. Gruesome, yes, but not as violent as a car crash, or being stabbed to death. I actually watched my grandfather go. It wasn't with a bang and a cloud of smoke like the term suggests. A cold blue flame hovered above his Christmas jumper, while he melted slowly from the belly upwards. Fat crackled and hissed as it oozed out of his broken flank onto the bedsheets below him; it nearly put me off meat for life. The smell of barbeques still sparks the memory. I never attend them, but if I'm out in the garden, or in the park, on a summer day, no doubt a reminder of my family's genetic defect, and my potential fate, comes wafting on the breeze and threatens to make me vomit.

After all these years the question of why I didn't run for help still lingers, but I was only five years old; I was in shock. The memory has become slightly muddled as time has passed. Sometimes I think his eyes were open, and other times he snored through the whole thing. One thing I'm sure of, is by the time my dad came into the room there was nothing left of Granda but his hands and feet, and a large gooey silhouette where he'd been lying.

Granda had been staying with us for Christmas and had gone for a nap after Christmas dinner. Dad and me (mostly Dad) had to push him up the stairs, as if we were shifting a sofa. Granda asked me to fetch him a glass of Bushmills so he could have a wee drink when he woke up. Dad poured it for me downstairs, but told me that Granda wasn't well and needed his rest, and I wasn't to be keeping him awake chatting. On my way up the stairs, I thought about tasting the whiskey, but the fumes made my eyes water. There was too much chance of an adult catching me, if it made me cough like I'd seen it do to people in films. I tiptoed up in case Granda was already sleeping. Inching the spare room door open only made it squeak, so I turned the handle and flung it open. Granda was on top of the bedsheets, fully clothed and on fire. I don't know how long I stood in the doorway watching him disappear, but I was transfixed the entire time. It was only when his head caught fire that I started to scream. In this version of my memory, his lips curled up at the side into a smile, half sinister, half smug.

That wasn't the last time someone in our family spontaneously combusted in that house. Following Granda's death it became a sort of pilgrimage for weirdos, UFO hunters and paraphysicists writing wonky books. They would travel from miles away just to stand at our front door and listen to shouts of 'fuck off,' every time they knocked. A few tried approaching Dad when he left for work, or when the family was out shopping. He only spoke to them to warn them what would happen if they tried to speak to me. Dad had been a boxer in his youth, and missed it. Despite what he thought of The Tin Foil Hat Brigade, as he called them, Dad himself believed that Granda's death was spontaneous combustion. My Uncle Eugene thought his bad heart could have given out. If he'd dropped a cigarette, that could have started the fire. Granda's death became the main talking point in our family. Dad and Uncle Eugene quizzed me about it for years. The drunker they were the longer the interviews would last, covering every little detail, even things they'd been told

I couldn't remember. I think that's why my memories aren't precise; I started making things up to cover the gaps. Just small things really: there was a greenish tint to the flame; he did a loud fart midway; the room had a strange smell to it, like pear drops. I stopped lying when I realised Dad lapped up every new detail, as if it somehow confirmed Granda's death had been a mysterious scientific curiosity. But I hadn't seen Granda ignite, so I'd no idea how the fire started. Sometimes I thought Dad was right, sometimes Uncle Eugene. Mum never said what she thought, but she told them both to stop questioning me. They ignored her, until they found out about my nightmares. These had been slow to start, because, as I child, I didn't understand what spont-aneous combustion was at first, but the more I listened to Dad and Uncle Eugene, the more I started to worry we would all just randomly explode someday. I couldn't believe people's bodies just burnt up with no warning. In my dreams Dad would explode while driving the family car and we'd all crash and die. Or I'd explode while being told off at school. Mum would explode watching her soap operas and the characters onscreen would point out of the TV and laugh at her (that one was a bit weird).

Mum died a year later; it was her that crashed the car, a more everyday death. Dad took it hard, harder than with Granda. He'd always been a drinker, but now it got heavier. He let the house go to shit and lost his job as a janitor at my school. There was a big scandal when he got drunk in the teachers' toilets and hid beer bottles in the cistern. The other kids called him a tramp. That's how I started to see him.

The night he spontaneously combusted he'd fallen asleep in front of the television watching *Minder*. Dad fancied himself a geezer, like Terry McCann. Maybe he was before his body turned to dough. Lying sprawled in his armchair, he was every sheet to the wind and dead to the world. I'd seen him like that before, and each time my first thought was he was really dead. He had a bad heart like Granda. The doctor told him to quit the fags and the booze and to take some exercise. Dad didn't listen, and indulged in both so freely it was as if he was trying to prove a point about how much he could take. I turned the television off and shouted at him to wake up. He didn't stir. I shook him by the shoulder. Again no response. I kicked an empty beer can at his face and screamed at him. The can missed its mark, but clipped his ashtray, toppling it off the arm of the chair. Ash and fag butts spilled over the thighs of his scruffy jeans, the ones frayed at the bottom of the legs like smoker's lungs. Maybe now he'd throw them in the bin, but in reality he wasn't even likely to throw them in the wash. He really looked dead. Then he started to snore. The last time I spilled his ashtray he beat the face off me. I bolted out of the room and upstairs, pushing my bed against my door as a barricade. When I came down the next morning he was ashes. Again only the hands and feet were left.

I didn't know what to think, and phoned Uncle Eugene even before calling the police. I wasn't sure how they could help, or who could help. The police arrived after Eugene. He took charge of the situation and did the talking, while I sat stunned in the kitchen, offering to make cups of tea nobody wanted. The police seemed spooked, as if they didn't want to spend any more time in the house than they had to. One of them muttered something about *The Amityville Horror*, but he saw I'd heard and didn't say any more. They concluded that Dad's death wasn't suspicious: the coroner even wrote 'Spontaneous Combustion' on the death certificate. The second official occurrence ever in Ireland. Granda's had been recorded as an accident – smoking in bed. The Tin Foil Hat Brigade claimed it was the first case in the world of it happening twice in the same family, which led to more extreme weirdo's prowling around, asking if they could study my DNA.

Uncle Eugene, who didn't believe Granda had magically gone boom, believed it even less about Dad. When I moved in with him he said straight up he thought I'd murdered the pair of them. He was drunk at the time, not that he apologised when sober. I understood it was hard for him though, not just because he'd been close with Dad, but people in town had started avoiding us. They'd cross the street if they saw us coming. Rumours spread that we dabbled in black magic. We were bad luck, and that can rub off on folk. But at least Eugene took me in, due to a twisted sense of duty that ran in my family. I was fourteen when Dad died. Eugene said he'd let me stay until I turned sixteen, then I could get a job and fend for myself. I'd no other living relatives, but to be fair, neither had he.

Before Dad's death I'd begun leaning towards the idea that a dropped cigarette had killed Granda, that spontaneous combustions was a childish notion, with no science behind it. But when the doctor put it on Dad's death certificate I thought there had to be something to it after all, and if it did run in the family, I could be next. The fear numbed me to the reality that I was now an orphan. I dreamt about spontaneous combustion all the time, only more vividly than before. The dreams were all about me. Sometimes I'd go up in a puff of smoke, like a genie jumping back into a lamp, other times I'd run screaming through my school corridors dripping with fire. I was only managing about four hours sleep a night. Uncle Eugene should have taken me to see a doctor. But as far as he was concerned I could twist in the wind. My performance at school plummeted, but even my teachers didn't reach out to me; they all knew my situation. I couldn't wait to leave school when my exams were over. Uncle Eugene kept reminding me that's when I'd be leaving his house too. Sometimes I hoped I'd come down in the morning and find him all ashes, hands and feet. That became my way of talking about it. Eugene wouldn't let me talk to The Tin Foil Hat Brigade - Head Melters, he called them. Some of them had written books, which I borrowed from the local library. I could tell by the amount of stamps that we were a popular topic around town. The first time Eugene caught me reading one he tore it up and threw it in the fire. He refused to pay the fine and said that would put me from reading more shit. I just stole them instead. The books mostly favoured spookiness over science. Dad and Granda were often a chapter, or a paragraph, thrown in with the other unexplained mysteries. But, as strange as the books tried to make it sound, all known cases of spontaneous combustion involved drunks, the elderly, or people with low mobility – all of whom had been alone when the fires started – with evidence that they smoked in bed or had fallen asleep beside an open fire. There was always a source of combustion. With a sick stomach, I reasoned there could have been a lit butt in Dad's ashtray. The more scientific explanations I could get my hands on described something called the wick effect. This suggested that once the person was on fire, their fat would soak into any surrounding fabric, mostly their clothes, but in Granda's case also a bed, and in Dad's also an armchair. The fat would act the way candlewax does, allowing them to burn slowly; that's why their bodies were almost entirely incinerated. But if the fires started from cigarette butts, why did they just sit through them? Dad once flicked a lit butt at me in bad temper, and it stung like a wasp. There was no way you'd sleep through that, paralytic drunk or not. This was the aspect that puzzled me most, and convinced me that spontaneous combustion must be something medical, that some part of the brain, or consciousness, must shut down to allow it to happen.

When school finished I got a job at the local store; no summer holidays for me. The job was awful; I used nothing that I'd learned at school. All those exhausted years struggling to stay awake in class for nothing. I thought about writing my own book, travelling the world giving talks, letting myself get poked and prodded by scientists, even if it did mean associating with The Tin Foil Hat Brigade – anything would be better than stacking shelves.

Coming up to my first month's wage, Uncle Eugene told me that when it hit the bank I was out, and he'd been looking forward to seeing the back of my creepy arsonist arse for long enough. When he was sober he looked out flats to rent in the newspaper, and even offered to come view them with me to make sure I didn't get ripped off.

When I started, the store needed a new fire warden. Uncle Eugene said with me around they'd need one. I was glad that the fire training was in the next town; no one there knew who I was. I could imagine every local prick dining out on how they bumped into me training to be a fire warden. Most of the course was common sense. One aspect that was fascinating was how people acted strange when panicked. There were stories of people who burnt to death, trapped in rooms because they pushed against doors they should have pulled. We were shown a video of the Bradford City stadium fire.

People again acted peculiar: not clearing the stands in time, watching how other people acted before doing anything themselves, but what struck me most was a spectator on fire, walking across the pitch in a daze, not screaming, not flailing, but as if he was out for a stroll and had lost his way. The instructor said, contrary to what we'd seen in films, people on fire go into a state of shock, and act differently to how you might expect. The reason why Dad and Granda didn't budge, didn't shout for help, had finally been solved.

Eugene had my pay date marked out on a calendar in the kitchen. When I came home that last night, he cornered me in the hall, telling me to go upstairs and pack, because tomorrow I was out. He wobbled and frothed like an ape doing a dance. Flecks of spit landed on my cheeks. I wished I was big enough to knock him on his arse. He'd the weight to go down hard.

Rolled up bin liners were already laid out in my room for me to chuck everything in. I sat on the end of my bed wishing he'd leave, or he'd be the next member of the family to magically go puff.

Around eight I went downstairs to make dinner. Dad had taught me the basics of cooking when mum died. I mostly made my own meals after that. Uncle Eugene never so much as made me a cup of tea. The money he got from the government was supposed to feed and clothe me, but I think he kept a lot for himself. That money stopped when I left school. Not for the first time, there was no food in the kitchen. I found a few small broken chips in the bottom of a bag in the freezer. We didn't even have sauce.

In the living room, Eugene snored like a mourning pig. Maybe because him, Dad and Granda had been heavy drinkers, I'd no interest in alcohol. I'd never even tried it. Other teenagers who went drinking down the forest at weekends never invited me; I was considered weird, and not in a cool way. Standing over my fat drunk uncle, I cracked open his last beer, probably saved for when he woke up. The ring pull's loud metallic snap bounced off the walls. Even that didn't rise him. My tongue twisted as the first mouthful touched my taste buds. I wanted to spit the bitter pish over him. Instead, I swallowed it and took another swig. It was fizzy and sour, like lemonade with no sugar. I decided then that this would be my first and only drink. And considering that, I might as well have my only smoke. My uncle's twenty deck of Benson & Hedges sat on the battered coffee table. I lit a cigarette and took my first drag. Years of watching Granda, Dad, and Uncle Eugene smoke had shown me how to do it right. Suck on the butt, drawing the smoke into your mouth. Take the cigarette out of your mouth and keep breathing in. The clean air draws the smoke down into your lungs. I started to cough. The taste was worse than the beer, like a moth had turned to dust in my mouth. I washed it away with another slug of beer. The fag had more of a hit, making me dizzy. The spins, people round school called it. I took another drink. I'd had enough of the fag. My only fag and my only beer. These were the things that had killed people in my family, not magic voodoo bollocks. The fire training had confirmed that for me. Even though it was an accident, it had been me that killed Dad. There must have been a lit butt in that ashtray. Even though he was a fat tramp at the end, he'd been good to me when I was younger, even, at first, when mum died. His image had started creeping back into my dreams – Dad asleep on that armchair, fat oozing out of his burning belly, soaking into the cushions below, and that slow blue flame that had hovered above Granda, climbing up to Dad's unaware head.

Trampy Uncle Eugene had never been good to me, not really. The things he'd said about me when Dad died, and me only fourteen. He'd been half right, although I didn't know it at the time. That made me hate him more. I flicked the fag butt at him. It bounced off the chair beside his head and fell down the side of the cushion. I waited, watching, edging closer to the door; if he woke up I'd be out of the house in a shot. He snored on. I finished my beer, taking it slow, all the time looking for that blue flame. It didn't come. I went upstairs defeated, packed my bags and slept.

The next morning Eugene was still in the armchair – hands, feet and ashes. It took a minute for the sight of him to sink in. I was so giddy I had to take another minute to calm myself and prepare to play the confused, grieving relative for the police. The coroner, the same one who'd investigated Dad's death, signed off on another case of spontaneous combustion. I, of course, was invited onto talk shows. Newspapers wanted to interview me, but I asked for privacy. A few people were suspicious, but their voices were lost among the babble of the conspiracy theorists. In my early twenties, when I was skint and finally sick of stacking shelves, I co-wrote a book with one of The Tin Foil Hat Brigade. He was the one who shored it up with pseudo-science and mystery. Writing with him was a mixed bag. He knew I was doing it for the money, but he was still hooked. He believed every word I put in that book, asking me to run over the details of my story a thousand times – a story I had nailed down tight. It isn't the one I've told here. Over the years my opinion has swung from one extreme to the other, from going to bed at night wondering if I'll burn in my sleep, to feeling guilty about what I know I did. To cope, I try to convince myself there is something unique about my family: our genetics or our lifestyles. That I haven't caught fire proves to me I killed two people. Though I tell myself these things can skip a generation, I'm never satisfied with that, but I wonder how it would feel if I someday burnt up too. I imagine the thoughts that would flicker through my head in those moments, from panic to relief, as my pain-filled body disproves the guilty notion that's bothered me for years. Or maybe, shock would take over, and I'd quietly sit still, only half aware of what's happening, as that slow blue flame crawls up my body, while around my head the world melts into a strange, but forgiving place.

Roland Miles

Trespass

Watching my brother Tom as he lay dying was rather amusing. We were at a boarding school for boys in Sussex, Beedings Court, the type run by misguided and rather clumsy amateurs, two brothers, who had exited the war, like so many men, with little idea as to what to do next. I imagine that they had reviewed their options, assessed their prowess in Latin, Classical Greek and how to patrol no-man's land after dark and had alighted upon the idea of a boarding school, where such skills might best be put to use.

Major Hugh smelled of the Olympus cigarettes which arrived each term in lieu of one boy's fees. Major Neville smelled of perfume, of the heady orchids which he kept in his buttonhole. Major Hugh was a pot-bellied figure, in outline much like Alfred Hitchcock. Major Neville had a tall, thin frame which had, I was to discover many years later, made him one of the most successful dames in the history of the Footlights, under the choreographic tutelage of Dadie Rylands, who really knew how to glide in a frock. On account of this, perhaps, he showed a rare sensitivity when it came to costuming the annual outdoor Shakespeare production, performed on the front lawns of the school on the final evening of the Summer term. One glimpsed then a joy, which had perhaps eluded him for much of his adult life. It was said that there were tears in his eyes when I had spoken my lines to a silk and muslin-draped boy the previous year. 'How sweet the moonlight sleeps upon this bank!/Here will we sit and let the sounds of music/Creep in our ears.' Major Neville was, of the two, the most benign but they were both monsters.

In my four years at the school, from the ages of eight to twelve, I was beaten seven times by Major Hugh, most often for my deficiencies in Latin. It would have been six but for the fact that in class I once laughed aloud at the vocative, *Mensa*. O, table! Why, I could not grasp, would one wish to speak with a table? Another boy was sent to fetch Excalibur, a cane *rotan* which was Major Hugh's preferred choice for academic misdemeanours. Touching my toes and reciting the noun several times in its singular form, he made contact each time I reached the dative. My elder brother Tom was cannier and better at declension. He was beaten only twice in all his time at the school, the last in his final term, and the occasion stands out for me far more clearly than any of my own regular punishments.

The first time that Tom was beaten, he had been stealing walnuts. Wily for the most part, he had neglected to research thoroughly enough the object of his crime. Walnuts leave stains, as obvious as the exploding ink which banks are said to put into cash bags. The walnut shells had been discovered beneath the tree in the garden of the Small House where Major Hugh and Major Neville lived. Tom knew he was in trouble. He had scrubbed his blackened hands, without effect. Major Hugh had gathered the School in the dining room. Before him, at the head table, were the shells, in an untidy pile. 'Someone has been into the garden of the Small House to satisfy his nasty little desires.' Major Neville nodded sagely at his side. 'Our walnuts have been purloined.' Major Neville smiled. 'Greed is a sin. Those who sin incur the wrath of the Almighty.' Major Neville's resulting laugh was like an indrawn sneeze. Keen to stretch out the event, Major Hugh had explained his dilemma. 'What is my duty in this matter?' he asked us.

Several hands went up. 'To punish the thief, Sir?'

Major Hugh turned to Major Neville. They smiled grimly and returned their gaze to us. 'Thou shalt not what?' he shouted.

'Steal,' we chanted.

'What else?' Silence. 'What else?' None of us had a reply. 'Thou shalt not be caught,' declared Neville, in that Cambridge drawl now only heard from senior civil servants and wrinkled members of the House of Lords.

'The eleventh commandment,' added Major Hugh. 'We would be failing in our duty if we did not teach you the consequences of stupidity, and all school boys are stupid, are they not?' He ran his hand over his pullovered paunch. 'Are they not?' he shouted.

'Yes, Sir.'

He picked up both halves of a walnut shell and held them up. 'The walnut resembles the human brain, gnarled and channelled,' he said. 'This tiny object is about the size of the brain of a stupid boy.' Major Neville, at his side, snorted in appreciation. 'Put up your hands if you are a stupid boy.' We looked at each other and slowly raised a hand. 'Plural,' he barked. 'Both hands!' When we had all raised our hands, he left us there for five minutes, chatting quietly with his brother, ignoring us, savouring our discomfort. Once he was satisfied that this part of the game had run its course, he wandered slowly around the tables, scrutinising, demanding that hands were turned palms out for inspection. Discovering ingrained dirt, he sent a few boys from the room to go without their lunch. He stopped in time before Tom. I suspect that he had seen his target from the outset and had prolonged Tom's wait on purpose. 'What have we here?' he asked exaggeratedly, pulling Tom up by his blackened fingers from his seat. Tom squirmed in pain. 'A coal miner in disguise?' There was a snigger from the outer reaches of the room. 'Or could it be that you have been stealing?' He raised his voice: 'Your guilt is tattooed upon your

fingers, Sir! Proceed to my study and fetch Joyeuse!'
Joyeuse was Major Hugh's second weapon, a rod *kanon*,
reserved for out of classroom crime. Tom rose from his
seat and left. We knew what was expected of us. We
began a drumming of our feet on the ground.

As Tom returned, we took up the chant which we
had learned at previous public floggings: 'Magister
puerum verberat!' we had to call out as our heels
banged rhythmically against the woodblock floor.
'Magister puerum verberat! Magister puerum verberat!'
The master beats the boy! The master beats the boy!
Holding back his tears, Tom was made to shake Major
Hugh's hand at the end of his punishment. Major
Neville stood with his own hands behind his back, a
smile of satisfaction upon his face.

In an age when children's safety was secondary to a
belief in the virtues of fresh if not freezing air, we were
expected to stay out in the grounds until bedtime long
after the end of Summer. We ranged over the twenty
acres without adult supervision, fighting mock wars,
defending territories and frequently taking our lives into
our hands. Our battlegrounds were the summerhouse
woods, the stable woods and the infinitely more
exciting lake woods. We spent hours precariously
shinning out on branches overhanging the lake,
creeping up on moorhens in order to scare them,
screeching Tarzan calls as we climbed through the
monkey puzzlers, and leaping in and out of the font
which lay in the heart of the Gothic folly, a *faux* abbey
ruin. One place to which we did not venture was the
island. This lay to one side of the lake, with a thin
bridge connecting it to the crumbling bank. Overgrown
and rotten, the bridge was untouched by us. On the
island were the fading sandstone graves of generations
of family pets; dogs which had belonged to the family

who had owned Beedings Court when it was a thriving estate. The graves, hemmed in by clusters of delicate, rare and supposedly deadly poisonous flowers, could be glimpsed across the stretch of water. Major Neville had hinted at the dangers of the island on several occasions. The bridge was cursed, of that we boys were sure. A hole in the rotting timbers, at the very centre of the bridge, was supposed to have been the scene of a terrible accident when a boy had tried to walk across- another tale delivered to wide-eyed new boys in the fresh gullibility of their first term. This last story was neither confirmed nor denied but allowed for years to rest uncomfortably in our imaginations. What is sure is that Major Neville was very fond of the plants and flowers which grew on the island. He had once given a lecture to the school about his love of orchids, a tedious self-aggrandising monologue, complete with slide show of rare and exotic types, some, he said, flowering only every thirty years, in which he painted himself as the saviour of species. 'I will not have rough boys trampling over my orchids. They are my lovelies.' He could be seen, on occasion, in the company of earnest scientific-looking types with long-lens cameras, pointing across at the island, windmilling his arms and snorting excitedly. We boys could not have cared less.

For some weeks after his beating, Tom withdrew into himself. He would sit on top of the rusting peacock cage at the edge of the lake woods, and stare resentfully back at the main house.

'Surveying' was the term which Tom devised to describe any activity which involved being out of bounds. Each term, there would be a moment when boredom set in and Tom would turn and smile at me. 'Well, Captain Oates,' he would say. 'Ready for another expedition?' We had walked the stable woods after midnight, creeping out past the caretaker's parrot cage by the outer door. We had explored the cellars, whose only attractions were a covered well, a defunct bread oven and a huge white marble bath, the latter intriguing enough to look at, to sit in once or twice, but limited in its entertainment value. We had broken into the costume cupboard, accessed via its own staircase to the side of the stables, full of musty cloaks, felt hats with long feathers, bags full of tights and buckled shoes. There were racks of dresses too, rather shabby in close up but which, as we saw each Summer, came to life under the spotlights which lit the outdoor stage as dusk approached. And there were the roofs which, towards the end, drew Tom so often out of the window on to the gully by our dormitory. The roofs were the last of Tom's great surveying discoveries and he came upon their possibilities by chance. We were sitting together on top of the peacock cage one evening when he said suddenly, 'When there were no more lands to conquer, man turned his sights upon the moon.'

'I don't understand,' I said.

'I'm bored by the woods. I'm bored by surveying. I want to climb.' He pointed to a tree which towered high above the rest on the front lawn. 'Are you ready, Captain Oates?' Braver than I, Tom clambered from branch to branch, reaching the highest part within ten minutes. I remained ten feet below him, where the trunk was solid. He sat, his knees clasped against the narrow tip, waving his arms above his head. We were so high up that the breeze caught his hair, lifting it. I had the illusion that he was flying. Waving and laughing, he spread his arms as if the same thought was running through his own head.

Suddenly, Tom became still. 'We need to measure this,' he said at last.

'What?'

'Last one down is a ....' His final word was lost in my panic as he clambered down over me. I watched him as he slipped swiftly and assuredly down the trunk and reached the bottom a good minute before I did. As I dropped from the lowest branch, I saw him heading off to the stables.

'Wait!' I called but he was too intent to notice. I ran after him and caught up as he negotiated the lock on the costume cupboard. He knew exactly what he was looking for. I had barely entered before he pushed back past me with a tape measure in his hand; a pink five-foot tape measure which Major Neville had more than once used in advance of the school play to measure heads, chests and inside legs. Within a couple of minutes, we were back at the foot of the tree. My lasting memory of the next hour is of the soles of his Clarks Commandos, the dangling pink measure, and his barked orders to, 'Pull the tape tight!' Give or take a small margin of error, Tom was able to declare with some authority that the tip was '108 feet from the ground.' Having announced the figure, Tom showed no inclination to move, basking in the sun, and perhaps glory, with his eyes closed.

'What next?' I asked.

'Enjoy the moment,' he said without opening his eyes. I waited another minute or two, then prepared to climb down. He clicked his fingers at me and I looked up.

'What is it?' I asked. No answer. 'Has someone spotted you? Tom, answer me!'

'Look!' he said, pointing towards the school buildings. His eyes were open now, staring. I looked down. The highest part of the line of the roof was well below us, well below even the halfway height of the tree.

'We ought to go down. Someone might see you.'

'Look!' he said again, more urgently. I followed the direction in which he was pointing, across the muddled roofs of the main buildings to the highest points of each apex. His fingers punched at the air, pointing down at the spiral-bricked chimneys. 'What do you think that is. And that? And that?' Before I had time to answer, he was away, once again overtaking me recklessly and with a laugh. 'You'll be late for the audition!' he called up as he accelerated down the trunk. 'See you there!'

'Audition' suggests an element of free will. We had been ordered to report for role allocations by Major Neville beneath the rotunda on the front lawn where the Summer play would eventually be performed. Failure to attend play meetings would lead to his adding you to the list of names passed to his brother for punishment, usually a beating at which he stood by. Major Neville never beat boys himself. He enjoyed watching.

We had no idea as to which play had been chosen nor were we particularly interested. It would be Shakespeare. Again. And there is nothing more tedious to the young than Shakespeare in the wrong hands. In much the same way that many schools choose their sports teams, dishing out wicket-keeping gloves and goalkeeper's jerseys without regard for size, weight or talent, so were parts distributed at Beedings Court. I had, the previous year, played a young lover wooing then eloping with Shylock's daughter. I had clearly impressed, for I had received a special mention from the visiting drama prize judge, a smarmy television actor who had been at the school in its infancy. He drove up in a cream-coloured Bentley moments before the performance began, delivered some words of wisdom briefly at the end, awarded a prize to the best actor, and escaped as soon as he could.

There was no buzz of excitement as we sat on the grass in front of Major Neville, just that same undercurrent of fear that we all felt in his presence. 'This year's play is one of the sweetest, one of the most delicious pieces ever written by the great bard,' began Major Neville. 'It is both comedy, haw-haw, and tragedy.' Puckering up his flabby mouth, he began to recite: '"My lips, two blushing pilgrims, ready stand to smooth/That rough touch with a tender kiss." For one night, one glorious Summer's evening, you can share the magic of this pretty language.' He stopped and ran his hand through his thinning hair. 'Which play?' he barked.

A few hands were hesitantly raised. '*Macbeth*, Sir?'

'Stupid child!'

'*A Midsummer's Night Dream*?'

'The title is *A Midsummer Night's Dream*. Do not misplace the apostrophe. And no, of course it is not the *Dream*. Although I may consider you for the role of Bottom in next year's play, haw-haw.'

We waited as he savoured the moment. '*Romeo and Juliet*!' he announced gleefully. 'A play which I have not directed for twenty-two years! What a treat it will be! Star-crossed lovers, warring families and sword fights aplenty. This production will be the best I have ever staged; mediaeval Italian costumes, yards and yards of flowing silks for the ladies and codpiece and hose for the gentlemen. Such a sight you will all be! Beautiful.' He was lost in his own vision for a moment; in the realm he loved best. 'Now, to business! The cast will now be revealed.' He drew out a long, thin sheet of paper from his jacket pocket. 'Mercutio will be played by Baines. Look pleased, Baines. It is a gift of a part. You will follow Olivier and Gielgud and Ralph Richardson, darling Ralph, in the role. You will be a star.'

'Thank you, Sir.'

'Romeo will be played by Fitch.'

I looked up. 'Which Fitch, Sir?' I asked.

'You, Sir! he replied. 'Fitch Junior. A fitting sequel to your Lorenzo, I am quite sure. And Juliet, dear Juliet, by Fitch Senior,' he added, looking at Tom. The details of the rest of the cast were lost in my bewilderment and by the muttering of Tom, sitting next to me.

'I'm not playing a ruddy girl,' said Tom beneath his breath. 'I'm not playing a ruddy girl!'

At last, Major Neville finished. Tom was still immersed in his fury, oblivious for the moment to his surroundings. I looked up and saw Major Hugh making his way across the lawn. Joining Major Neville, he held out his hand for the sheet of paper on which the cast was written.

'I'm not playing a ruddy girl.'

Major Hugh looked up. 'What did you say, young man?'

Tom held his silence for a moment. 'I don't want to play a girl,' he said defiantly.

'What did you say, young man?' he repeated, with that touch of menace which he had practised so often.

Tom held the silence for a moment too long. 'Nothing, Sir,' he said finally.

We sat on the roof, outside the dormitory window, in an area enclosed on all sides by slate slopes. Tom was still smouldering, so it was unexpected when he suddenly said, 'That's what I meant,' pointing to the apex of the roof. 'And that.' I looked up. At each corner of the several roof expanses, almost at the level of the top of the chimneys, was a small rounded lead cupola from which spiralled a thin twisting piece of decorative wood. Tom pulled himself up and placed his feet carefully into the narrow rising gully, his hands steadying himself on the surrounding tiles. He edged up to the top and straddled the ridge tile. Shinning his way out and across, he was soon near the far end of the protruding wing, a fifty foot drop to either side of him. He rose carefully, feet balanced on the rolled lead, and gripped the cupola in a hug. Unlike my own safe spot, out of sight and cushioned within the nest of roofs, Tom was in plain view to anyone looking up. He reached up and tentatively applied pressure between thumb and fingers. The wood was brittle and snapped easily. He held up the piece and smiled down at me. 'Number one,' he mouthed.

Once down, he lay back, leaning against the slope of the slates. He made me fetch my chess set from my locker, offering no explanation. When I returned, he was still in the same position, his eyes closed. The chess set was housed in a blue and silver Farrah's Harrogate Toffee tin. He emptied out my chess pieces. The spiral tip which he had broken off was the size of a small conker, no more. The wood was grey with age and the surface mottled, battered. He weighed it in his hand, dug his thumbnail into the fissures which ran down its length. Smiled. 'That's been up there a hundred and twenty years. There are seventeen of them; one on the top of each cupola. I mean to have the tip of every one of them. I reckon there's enough room for all of them in here, don't you?' He placed the tip in the tin and carefully closed the lid. 'The hard one will be the one on the top of the tower.' I looked across at where he was pointing. To the right-hand corner of the building was a thin, rather nonsensical spire. It had a four-sided capped roof and was covered, unlike the other roofs, in copper sheeting which had turned a patinated green over time. It was a good fifteen feet taller than the rest of the structure which surrounded it. At its zenith, as with all the other roofs, was a decorative lead cupola with a spiral of weathered oak. I could not see how one might gain sufficient purchase to make such a climb and told Tom so. He ignored my comment. 'Next expedition tomorrow, do you think, Captain Oates?' I gathered my chess pieces from the gully and followed him back through the window into the dormitory corridor.

I thought he would soon bore of it, but by the end of the week, he had placed several of the tips in the tin. It became a daily ritual, a dally with danger, as he pushed out towards the further reaches of the roof and gradually acquired his targets. As the close of term approached, the collection was almost complete.

There comes a point in a school production when all pretence at schooling is abandoned. We began to miss lessons on a daily basis in order to attend extra rehearsals. Long afternoons spent in direct sunlight on the outdoor stage became the norm. 'Bring it to life, boy,' hissed Major Neville at Tom from his deckchair. 'We are only three days away from the dress rehearsal and you are mumbling. Imagine yourself in the shoes of this delightful creature, swooning with first love, her Romeo filling her up with sweet, and not so sweet thoughts, haw haw. Let us glimpse the struggle within her innocent breast.'

Tom exchanged a glance with me: 'Ugh!'

'Good night, good night. Parting is such sweet sorrow,/That I shall say good night till it be morrow.' Tom slammed out the words in a monotone.

Major Neville rose angrily from his seat. 'You need

to try much harder or I shall speak with my brother.' He walked slowly towards us, stepped on to the low wall which separated the stage from the audience area and stopped in front of Tom. He was so close that I could smell the slightly rotten scent of the flower in his lapel. 'Make an effort,' he snarled. 'Most girls would die for a role like this. Haw, haw.'

Dress rehearsals are supposed to go wrong. It is one of the legends of the theatre that a rotten dress rehearsal is succeeded by a wonderful first night. We were due to put on our costumes after lunch and spend the afternoon running through wobbly scenes and firming up entrances and exits before the final rehearsal under the lights in the evening. 'The descending darkness of the night will echo the darkness of the events taking place on stage,' Major Neville had explained to us earlier in the week. 'This is known as pathetic fallacy.' The day, however, began unexpectedly, and the plans which had already been announced were turned on their heads. We were called back into the dining room first thing in the morning for an announcement. Major Hugh and Major Neville stood at the front as we filed silently in.

'I have an important announcement to make,' said Major Neville. 'My brother will oversee events this afternoon and even, perhaps, this evening.'

'Today is a momentous day,' added Major Hugh. 'My brother is to be recognised for an achievement which he has been seeking all his life.'

'Today,' said Major Neville, 'we are to be visited by the British Broadcasting Corporation. They are coming down from London to film at our school and to interview me.'

'My brother,' continued Major Hugh, 'has succeeded in cultivating a flower on the island which was declared extinct many years ago. I believe a round of applause would be in order for this exceptional moment.' We rose as was expected and clapped with a semblance of enthusiasm. Major Neville pulled himself upright with pride. His face and bald head reddened and he winced. I realised after a moment that he was attempting a smile.

Eventually, he raised his hand and the room quietened. 'This is the first sighting of the Wraith Orchid for nearly thirty years and it has just flowered. It is a strongly fragrant flower, with a single blossom in the shape of a spreading bell. It is a perfectly beautiful gentle pink in colour with tiny blood red speckles at its throat. It is a delight.' Tom rolled his eyes at me. 'You will be able to see it, and me, on your television sets in a special programme during the approaching holiday. This is such an exciting day. The zenith of my achievement as a horticulturalist.'

'Therefore,' said Major Hugh, 'We shall have some very important visitors this afternoon from the BBC Natural History Unit, so I expect all members of the school to be on their best behaviour.' He was back to the hectoring tone to which we were used. 'I shall be taking the rehearsals whilst my brother looks after the BBC. I shall expect you to work hard to iron out the creases in your performances. Otherwise, Joyeuse will need to make an appearance on the stage with you. Is that clear?' The buzz of excitement which had erupted at the mention of the BBC was quickly suppressed at the threat of the cane.

The BBC van arrived at lunchtime. We were almost hanging out of the windows, eagerly watching its arrival. Major Neville was waiting at the front of the school, a fixed grin on his face. He had dressed up; a red velvet jacket topped by a silk cravat. When they drove up, it was something of a disappointment. Two men and a woman got out, all quite young. They were dressed in what looked like hiking gear. I suppose I had imagined something more polished, more glamorous. The woman lugged the camera and tripod out of the van. The first man carried a heavy black case. The second man, who was carrying a megaphone, seemed to be in charge, so Major Neville went immediately over and shook his hand energetically. We could see him bowing and laughing, keen to make a good impression. The four of them set off towards the island.

'Chop chop,' said Major Hugh, entering the room. 'Get down from those windows at once and into your costumes.'

'This dress is scratchy,' complained Tom to me, 'and I hate wearing stockings.'

'I have to wear stockings as well.'

'Not under a petticoat and skirt. I look like an idiot,' he said. 'Just look at this stupid bow on the waist.'

'It isn't your colour either,' I added. He looked across at me sharply. Then he laughed.

'Out on to the lawn,' ordered Major Hugh. 'Two minutes.'

It was a tedious afternoon, a rehearsal for the dress rehearsal, with constant stops and starts. 'No, no, no. We will do that again until you can manage it properly.' Whatever minor subtleties Major Neville had achieved in earlier sessions, Major Hugh killed stone dead. It was as if he was ordering troops around a battle field. 'Not there, foolish child! Two steps to the left!' he bellowed. 'Thrust! Thrust! It's a sword not a feather duster!' he thundered. 'Kiss him as if you mean it, boy!' he roared.

It was only when I was being made to run through the opening of Act V again and again that I noticed that

Tom had slipped away. I looked around but could see him nowhere. I was having to concentrate on my own lines at the same time but it was not hard to shine standing alongside Balthasar or the apothecary, who were both as static as lumps of wood. 'You are delivering news of a heart-wrenching death, you stupid boy, not reciting a shopping list! Do it again,' shouted Major Hugh. Balthasar burst into tears. Nor was I immune from criticism: 'The line is, "Come, cordial and not poison, go with me/To Juliet's grave; for there must I use thee." He is going to kill himself. Don't say it as if he's announcing a visit to the lavatory.'

I looked around again but there was still no sign of Tom. He was due on stage within minutes, albeit as a dead body, or a body pretending to be dead. He still needed to be on stage, though.

Glancing across the lawns, I saw Major Neville heading towards us, camera crew in tow. He stopped with his back to us and the woman set up her camera on the tripod. The sound man stood with his microphone on a long pole held above. The director stood behind them all. We were to be the backdrop. Before, however, the interview could begin, Major Neville began to shout. All action on the stage stopped and we, and Major Hugh, looked across to see what had caused the commotion. Major Neville appeared to be attacking the director.

'Neville, dear boy,' called Major Hugh. 'Steady on!' We all moved forward as he went towards his brother so that we could hear what was being said. Major Neville had wrestled the megaphone from the director. 'What in heaven's name is going on?' asked Major Hugh to no-one in particular.

'There's a girl hanging from your roof, Sir,' said the director. Major Neville wrenched the megaphone from the director's hand and started bellowing into it. The director leant across. 'You need to press that button at the same time as you talk.'

'I know that!' said Major Neville, angrily. 'You boy. Come down at once!' he shrieked. This time his voice echoed across the lawns.

'I am almost sure it's a girl,' the BBC man said anxiously.

'It's a boy, you blithering idiot. We only have boys in this school.'

We looked up. Major Neville and Major Hugh looked up. Hanging from the very top of the tower was Tom, his legs scrabbling furiously to gain a hold on the gutter. He was caught on the edge of the copper roofing, his dress snagged. 'Down, boy!' shouted Major Hugh, as if he wouldn't get down if he was able. Suddenly, he gave a cry. There was a loud tearing sound. The guttering seemed to come away in slow motion. It curled gently sideways and Tom disappeared from view. There was a collective gasp from everyone. All I could do was watch helplessly. Major Hugh and Major Neville rushed towards the main building.

He was not dead. He was rather battered and certainly subdued as I discovered when I was called into Major Hugh's study. Tom was sitting on a hard chair in the corner. He had a graze on his cheek and a large rip in his skirt which ran from front to back. Both brothers were standing. On the desk was the Farrah's Harrogate Toffee tin, its lid sitting on the blotter. I looked at Tom and he shook his head. As I came in, Major Neville shut the door and stood with his back resting against it.

'It is clear to us that you were both involved in this silly venture,' began Major Hugh.

Tom began to protest but was silenced by a growl from Major Neville. 'Silence, you loathsome creature.

How dare you spoil today. Today was my day. How dare you...how dare you...' He was lost for words.

Major Hugh reached down to the elephant foot umbrella stand which he kept by his desk. In it nestled Joyeuse and Excalibur. 'Joyeuse,' I thought. 'He is going to beat Tom with Joyeuse.'

There was a knock at the door. Major Neville turned and opened it a fraction. 'Not now,' he shouted without looking and slammed it shut.

'Up,' said Major Hugh to Tom. 'Hands on ankles.' Tom did as he was told.

There was another knock at the door. 'Clear off. I've already told you once,' shrieked Major Neville throwing the door wide open.

Waiting at the door was a startled looking BBC director, the camerawoman and sound man just behind. He coughed in an embarrassed way. 'I was wondering whether we might do that final interview?' His eyes drifted beyond Major Neville to Major Hugh, to the cane in his hand, to Tom standing defenceless in front of him, bending down, giant rip in petticoats and skirt, stockinged buttocks exposed. 'I say,' he said. 'You can't treat children like that. It's not right.'

'Don't tell me what I can or can't do in my own school, you jumped-up worm,' snapped Major Hugh. 'Why don't you go back to your cosy little BBC world and leave us to deal with matters which do not concern you?' He was waving Joyeuse threateningly as he spoke. The spray of spittle from his mouth was caught in the sunlight from the window.

There was suddenly a look of panic in Major Neville's eyes. 'He doesn't mean it,' he said. 'I'm sure we can do the interview now. Just give me a minute.'

The director looked round at his companions then turned back to Major Neville. 'That will no longer be necessary,' he said. 'We have to be going.'

'But my orchid,' pleaded Major Neville.

'What orchid?' replied the director and headed towards the front door. Major Neville began to whimper.

Major Hugh beat both of us. He beat Tom until he cried. Nine strokes. It was unheard of.

Tom was given a new costume. Major Hugh could not resist a snide remark: 'It is very unbecoming in a young lady to have her drawers on show so we shall find you something else pretty to wear.' The dress rehearsal went ahead as planned. Major Neville was still in a daze so Major Hugh had once again taken the reins. Tom was awful. He mumbled, forgot lines and appeared late on stage. In the crypt scene, in which he had to pretend to be dead, he started to laugh, inexplicably and uncontrollably. Major Hugh, defying every protocol which said that the show must go on without interruption, stopped the final scene mid-way and climbed up on to the stage. 'You must not corpse on stage. Laughing puts off your fellow actors,' he shouted.

'But I am a corpse,' he whispered to me as I leant over him. 'If a corpse can't corpse, then who can?'

Major Hugh was intent on finishing his lecture: 'An actor who corpses will never work again. You have compounded an embarrassing and outrageous act with an absolute no-no of the theatre.' The word 'no-no' set Tom off again. We got through the play somehow. Major Hugh was in vicious mood. Most of us were rather bewildered and not a little nervous of the next day. If it is an axiom that a poor dress rehearsal presages a wonderful first night, then we were on to a winner.

It was extraordinary that the next day began as if

nothing untoward had happened. Major Hugh kept us behind after breakfast and ran tediously through the events for the day. 'Clear the boot rooms. Empty your lockers. Check the lost property box. Pack your trunks. Collect your tuckboxes from the cellar. Everything is to be stored in the small hall for your parents to pick up and load into their cars before the play this evening.' As soon as the play was finished, we were reminded, our parents had to sweep us off the premises as quickly as possible. 'Headmasters need their holidays as well,' said Major Hugh. Major Neville stood sombrely in the background.

The morning was something of a free for all. Luggage went up and down stairs, paint was chipped from walls and the noise level betrayed an underlying excitement at the thought of escape. The usual rule about running in the corridors was abandoned and no-one was inclined to admonish with the usual cry of 'We are a walking school!'

We played board games after lunch. Whilst others in the school were then pushed out of doors to fill their lungs with air, those in the cast were confined to dormitories for a 'rest' in advance of the big performance. An early supper was followed by makeup and the putting on of costumes.

Parents began arriving at 7.00pm. Those of us in the cast were not allowed to see our parents until after the play so we watched from a distance. I spotted my mother and father arriving but they were soon absorbed into the crowd. Drinks and canapés had been laid on and were being carried around on trays by waiters and waitresses who had been hired in for the evening.

There is no more public show of a school's worth than a school play so Major Hugh and Major Neville were on hand to shake hands and to cosy up to the parents with the most expensive cars. With half an hour to go before curtain up, we were all lined up behind the yew hedge which skirted the back of the stage, peeping through the gaps. There was suddenly a hush. Through the crowd danced a very old and rather dapper man who was immediately pounced upon by Major Neville. 'Ladies and gentlemen!' he chanted in an excited voice. 'May I introduce to you the distinguished writer, Mr Ronald Wilson?' There was a burst of applause.

'Darling Hugh! Darling Neville! How good to see you,' he sang. It was the first time that Major Neville had looked cheerful all day. 'What a wonderful evening! What a super turnout! Such a loyal group of parents. Devotees of Shakespeare, all! What a treat we are in for - all thanks to my very talented friend, Neville!' Major Neville glowed with pride. 'Ah, thank you, my dear,' he said to an approaching waiter, lifting a Champagne glass from a tray.

'To your seats, ladies and gentlemen,' announced Major Hugh. 'We are about to begin.'

Adults take longer to herd than children so it was some minutes before they were seated. They were noisy too, far noisier than we would have been. It was only when Major Neville stepped up on to the stage and called for quiet, that a silence descended. 'It has been twenty-two years since I last had the privilege of putting on this bitter-sweet, enigmatic play...' he began. I switched off at that point. I had heard it all before.

It was only at the end of the first act that Tom and I met on stage for the first time as Romeo and Juliet. As I took Tom's hand and raised it to my lips, there was a collective sigh of delight from the audience. Ronald Wilson, sitting in the front row, clasped his hands together in glee. Alongside him, Major Neville was grinning broadly, his troubles momentarily forgotten.

By the halfway stage, I realised that the play was going well. Everyone seemed to have remembered his lines, the sword fights drew applause and the audience was laughing in the right places. Tom seemed to have recovered from the anger which had been eating him up since our departure from Major Hugh's study. There was an energy and playfulness in his performance as Juliet which he had not shown in any of the rehearsals. He seemed to be having fun.

As we neared the end of the play, the natural light gradually dimmed, as Major Neville had told us it would. The theatre lights took over, casting shadows behind us. It really did feel magical on that stage, cocooned within the yellow warmth of the spots and the yew hedge cyclorama. As the tragedy unfolded, I could feel the audience being swept up by the story, a story whose tragic ending they already knew, an ending which they were willing to be different.

'Ah, dear Juliet,/Why art thou yet so fair?' There was a sharp intake of breath as I lifted the poison bottle to my mouth: 'O true apothecary! Thy drugs are quick./Thus with a kiss I die.' I fell on to the platform which represented Juliet's tomb and on which Tom lay. My eyes half-closed, I could see the sadness in the reflected faces of the audience.

At the very moment at which I breathed my final breath, Tom raised himself up and cried out in anguish, a noise echoed by Ronald Wilson in the front row. 'What's here? A cup, closed in my true love's hands,' sobbed Tom. He leant over me and bent down for the final kiss, a kiss designed to steal the poison from my lips. All eyes were on him.

There was suddenly a shriek from the audience. 'Stop!' screamed the voice. 'This cannot go on!' It was Major Neville, up on his feet. Major Hugh was attempting to restrain him. Ronald Wilson was uselessly patting his hand.

Tom carried on: 'Yea, noise? then I'll be brief. O happy dagger!' he said, picking up the stage knife which I had carried on with me. He plunged it theatrically towards his padded chest. '...there rust and let me die.' There was a gasp from the audience as he slumped forward.

As he fell, I saw, through my half-closed eyelids, a pink bell-shaped flower in his hair, with what I could only assume were red speckles at its throat; the single, rare blossom of Major Neville's elusive Wraith Orchid. As Tom dropped back on the funeral bier, the flower was crushed, its petals exploding dramatically on to the ground. 'Nooooooooooo!' wailed Major Neville rising up, his arms outstretched. 'My lovely, my poor lovely!' he sobbed, collapsing back into his seat.

The closing minutes of the play passed in a chorus of sniffles from the audience. I cannot swear to the fact that Major Neville was amongst those actually weeping, but I think it very likely. I looked across at the prostrate Tom and saw him wink. Throughout the final speeches of the play, through the Prince's reprimand to the adult characters for their foolish behaviour toward the young people in the story, I could see Tom's chest rising and falling as he laughed silently, happy that he had affected his intended audience in exactly the way he had hoped.

I do not suppose that anyone, but for Major Neville and Major Hugh, had any idea as to what had really taken place. Ronald Wilson was clearly oblivious; as he made his speech at the end, Major Neville's suffering was made even more acute. 'And this year's prize for the best actor goes to Thomas Fitch for his entrancing performance as Juliet. What an inter-pretation and how beautifully he brought out the complexities of this tragic, bewitching creature.' At this point, he looked down towards his old friend, Major Neville. 'I was not the only one present whose soul cried out when she met her death. Some of us were overwhelmed. Bravo, young man! Bravo! Bravo!' There was huge applause as Tom came forward to collect his prize and shake the hand of his enthusiastic champion.

My father's delight in Tom's achievement was swiftly tempered by the discovery next day of the bruises which he had sustained from his beating. It had been Tom's final term. Our parents decided to take me away at the same time and place me in another school. My father described the behaviour of Major Hugh and Major Neville as 'shabby' and consulted his solicitor. He had some idea that Tom had not been entirely an innocent party, but could not forgive these old-fashioned men their cruelty.

The school closed down some three years later. I still think of the place fondly.

Meganrose Weddle

The Fish that was not my Pa

I knew the fish was not my Pa, because I caught it before he died. I could not sleep for the murmurings and for the knowledge that Pa was not going to make it past morning. The house was too warm – had been for weeks – and I lay there thinking about how nice it would be to wade into the shallows. The smell of Pa's legs, green and black and oozing, was made worse by the heat, and I thought of Daniel, who should be in his room but was likely in the back kitchen with the dog. That made me sit up and swing my legs out onto the floorboards. Even they felt warm and slick from the fire and the fever.

I could reach the back kitchen by creeping down the stairs and through what Pa still called the parlour, rather than passing down the hallway, where I was likely to be heard by a great mass of folks who'd been in the house since yesterday. I eased Daniel awake and led him from the fold-away cot he'd taken to sleeping in. The dog woke up but I hushed him and told Daniel to put his boots on, holding my finger to his lips so he knew to stay quiet. We kept in our nightshirts, but I lifted our coats and rods from the back porch, gently closing the screen door so as not to disturb the party gathered around the big bed in the sitting room.

That bed had been a wedding gift, and Pa, when he could still talk, had demanded it be brought down when he could no longer take the stairs. He'd said if Maw died in that bed then he would too. It had taken some six men to carry it down. They'd done it without grumblin' though. Pa was a good man – he'd helped many of them out of what Pa called 'sticky patches'. I did not know what that meant but I knew if I was ever stuck in the mud, I'd sure want Pa to pull me out.

'We goin' fishin' now, Bo?' Daniel mumbled as we turned off the road onto the path that led to the lake.

The night was humid, and the dark swelled into every space not two feet from our eyes, so's I felt as if we were walking in a rolling sphere of moonlight.

'Yea', baby. It's too hot to be sleepin'.' Daniel nodded in dazed agreement and trundled along next to me, rubbing his eyes with his knuckles. I felt sorry for waking him, but I thought of the house and what he would rise to come morning, and pressed on. We lived just a short walk from the lake's edge. Pa called it a lake but I had never seen the other side 'cept the mountains looming as if right out of the water, so I figured it may as well be the sea. Sometimes, if I lay real quiet in bed, I could hear geese running on the water. I often wished we lived close enough so's I could hear the sound of the tide lapping against itself.

It wasn't long before Daniel was sleeping among the rushes, wrapped in my coat and his. I sat still, inches from the shallow drop of the bank, one leg bent so's my knee could hold up my chin and the other making circles in the water. It was easier to see here than on the road because the moon shone so brightly on the lake's surface, and beyond were the mountains. They seemed to prop up the world like the bookends in Pa's study. They kept all the sky and the stars from tumbling over the edge, just so's I could see the end of my line.

I stayed some time gazing at the water, its gentle current teasing my mind into thinking the whole lake was edging closer and closer, when all the while it stayed just where it was. Where it had always been. And then, just as my own eyes were closing, a tug.

I snapped awake, two hands grasped on the line, and waited. For a moment, it was still and I was sure I'd lost the bite, or imagined it entirely. But then, another tug, this time stronger and I stood up quick as I could and began to reel him in. A glance at Daniel showed he had not stirred at my commotion, even though the reel seemed to be whirring so loud in my ears it could wake the whole town and the fish's splashes were the same as if I'd jumped right on in to catch him with my bare hands.

As it was, I had not the struggle I'd had with other fish. This one seemed not to strain so much against the line, but I was still careful not to let the line break by reeling it in too fast. Every few feet, I pulled my rod to see the shine of his curved back break the surface. Sometimes he'd turn on his side and I could see his belly, lighter than the rest, speckled like a duck egg. Two long whiskers drifted from his snout so I knew what kind of fish he was. Pa said those whiskers were called baubles, like the Christmas decorations, or something like that. I could not remember exactly. Pa hadn't taken us fishin' in a while.

When I got it into the shallows, I waded in past my ankles. I felt the mud swirling over my skin and shimmied my heels in as deep as I could so's to keep anchored. I brought in the last few yards of line so's the fish was swimming 'bout me. I could tell the fish was four-foot-long from nose to tail and what looked a dark blue, like the sky at the base of the mountains beyond. I left him hooked, but comfortable, in the lapping water. Daniel slept on. I was pleased to be alone, and after some time bent down and cradled the creature, stroked it and let it drift through the current. It did not try to wriggle free of my hands where I held it, but instead seemed to sort of rest against me, so's I felt the weight of the fish even in the water. Sometimes those baubles tickled my arms and the fish would turn quickly, its muscular body bending at the trunk. Eventually I eased the fish between my ankles but was sure not to leave so narrow a gap that he could not float freely. The fish seemed just fine to stay that way.

I stood like that a long time. I let the silt creep up my ankles and prayed my legs would not one day turn like Pa's. As the night began to melt I could see that the fish was not blue, but a dark and mottled green turning to white at the belly.

Ivan came running around the time Daniel began to stir.

'Who's that, Bo?' Daniel whispered. 'Do you think—'

'Baby, I think whoever it is, we must be brave.'

Daniel nodded, and climbed to his feet. He shook his head vigorously as he did so.

It had grown cold but I stayed fixed in the water, holding the fish between my legs, as the running boy reached us. I had to turn my upper half to face the shore and our future.

Ivan was almost grown and determined to be a man. He crunched sand underfoot as he shuddered to a stop, and looked in my eyes when he said it.

'Robert, your father is dead.'

'When?' I said.

'Just now. Just as the birds started singing.' Ivan lifted a skinny wrist and gestured to the lightening horizon.

Daniel let out a sharp whine, like an animal caught in a trap, then stamped his foot once, and then again, on the sand about the rushes. I think he was trying to hold it all in.

'Maw says the birds carried him off. When she saw you was out of yo' beds, she said to go lookin'.'

We were silent then, and I turned back to the expanse of water before me. The fish swayed gently against the bony point of my ankles, sending tremors to the surface. I looked down at the bubbles, then back at the two boys on the bank. When he saw the fish bobbing in the arch of my legs, Ivan's tongue darted across his bottom lip and he glanced from me to Daniel and back again.

'Who caught the mudcat?'

'Daniel,' I said. Daniel made to protest, then thought better of it and rubbed his toe in the sand. 'I'm just holdin' it for 'im.'

'Whoa, he's a beauty. Did you catch him just now?' he said to Daniel. Daniel made to say something, but I answered for him.

'Just now,' I lied, although I did not know why. Daniel knew better than to move.

Ivan ran after that, to tell those awake of the fish and of Daniel. Ivan's maw was very religious. Ivan was trained to accept signs of the Great Father and he'd seen one first-hand. Daniel and I stood silently and watched the horizon turn a pale pink at its base. I could feel Daniel's shoulders trembling, though he stood on the bank.

'Daniel,' I said, without turning to face him.

'Yea', Bo?'

But I did not know what to say in that moment. I heard Bo's feet in the water before I felt his hand in mine. I squeezed it hard and bent to kiss the top of his head, careful not to move my legs. In his free hand, Daniel held the steel bucket, which bobbed on its side next to him. We had become so in tune with the world around us in the preceding hours that the squeaking of the handle was eerie in the stillness. After some time, we slowly scooped the fish into the bucket, tail first.

It was an extraordinary fish; it was so still. Its pupils were small but seemed to take in everything. I had been sure to let it recover from the catch, so I knew it was neither tired nor dying. On our walk back in the milky dawn, each holding one handle of the squeaking bucket so as not to let the slippery knot of the fish slop over the sides, I told Daniel to say he caught the fish.

'Really?' he squealed, then hesitated. 'But, it's not right Bo. You caught the fish. It's too big for me; no one will believe it.'

'They'll believe,' I said.

As we turned from the path onto the road, I could see those who had been with my father in his final rasping hours sat about the front porch. The house was dark but for a candle burning in Pa's room, and Ivan's maw was singing from somewhere in the shadows. The song drifted down to the men, who smoked in silence.

Ivan was quivering at the corner of the road, in front of the house. I think he had been too nervous to break the men's silence without proof. When he saw us, he bolted across the yard and, although I could not hear the words, I knew he was telling of his finding us, that we knew of Pa's passin', and of the fish.

The men's heads turned to follow Ivan's pointing finger. The bucket was heavy so I signalled to Daniel to set it down where we stood and waited for the men to meet us.

The men walked over as one mass, and one picked up the fish, which thrashed and slapped against chest and arm, gulping and staring from the two tiny points on the side of its bony head. The fish's long whiskers ran from grey-green to white at the tips. Someone joked that my Pa's hair was grey and white. Someone else said that my Pa had come back in the form of the fish and therefore we must throw the fish back into the lake so my Pa could live again. One man took it by the tail and it dangled there, wriggling so strong it almost met its tail with its mouth, until the man placed the struggling fish back into the bucket.

'Ivan says Daniel caught it,' the man who was sure my Pa was in the fish said to me.

'Yes,' I said.

The man's face seemed to worry itself into a look I did not recognise and I was not sure if he believed me. But then he picked up Daniel and let him ride on his broad shoulder. The men gathered in a circle and began to sing, passing Daniel from man to man as they did so. I was sure the ruckus would wake up the whole town but the men seemed not to mind if it woke up the whole world. I turned to make the walk back to the lake alone. I was tired and the bucket was difficult to lift on my own. But I was pleased we would not kill the fish. Even though I knew it was not my Pa.

Daniel looked back as I was lifting the bucket, his forehead bunching into a frown. I tipped my cap and turned away. Daniel would be King for a day. And I hoped he would remember his ride on the shoulders of men rather than rotten legs and rasping.

When I got back to the water's edge, it was almost full daylight. The fish was still again, curled in the bucket, and I wondered if it was called a catfish not for its baubles but for the way it rolled up into a coil. But then I remembered this fish was not yet a free fish and would not always be curled up like this.

I stroked the fish for a while as it lay in the bucket. I ran my fingers along its whiskers, which were soft and bendy. I looked at the white tips, carefully holding them between my fingers in front of my eyes. I could see that, close up, they were speckled too, like its belly, where the white dotted into green. They were not like my Pa's hair at all, but more resembled flakes of snow on the top of the mountains beyond. The small eyes stared from the depth of the bucket but the fish remained still. I carefully lifted its head out and pulled the mouth open and shut, watching the hinge expand and retract. With the mouth wide, I could see through the gills and back into the lake. This fish did not belong in a man's belly nor in a boy's bucket. I knew that but I did not want to know it.

Eventually, squatting with one knee either side of the bucket, I dipped my arms into the steel bowl and pulled the fish out, hugging it tight so as not to drop it. The fish was heavy and I had to lean back slightly to stay balanced as I stepped into the shallows. I sat down in the water and held the fish. I ain't 'shamed to say I cried somewhat. And then I let the fish go.

It hesitated for a moment, and then dissolved into the murky water. I lifted my legs out: they were covered in greenish silt and weeds from where I'd been sitting in the shallows. I felt glad that I could wash that green stuff off. I felt glad that the fish was free.

Notes on Contributors

Dr Tanvir Bush is a novelist and film-maker/photographer. Born in London, she lived and worked in Lusaka, Zambia, setting up the Willie Mwale Film Foundation, working with minority communities, street kids and people affected by the HIV/AIDS pandemic. Her feature documentary 'Choka!- Get Lost!'. was nominated for the Pare Lorenz Award for social activism in film in 2001. She returned to UK to study and write and her first novel *Witch Girl* was published by Modjaji Books, Cape Town in 2015. She is the designer and facilitator of the Corsham Creative Writing Laboratory initiative and an Associate Lecturer at Bath Spa University in Creative Writing. She is based in Wiltshire with her guide dog and research assistant, Grace.

Maureen Cullen lives in Argyll & Bute. She has been writing poetry and short fiction since 2011 after early retirement from her social work career. In 2016, she was published, along with three other poets, in *Primers 1*, a collaboration between Nine Arches Press and the Poetry School. She won The Labello Prize for short fiction in 2014, and has stories published in Gem Street, Scribble, Prole, the Hysteria Anthology, the Evesham Anthology, Leicester Writes Anthology, Stories for Homes Volume 2, and online at Ink Tears. Her stories have been longlisted and shortlisted at various competitions.

Raphael Falco is a Professor of English at the University of Maryland, Baltimore County where he held the 2012-2013 Lipitz Professorship of the Arts, Humanities, and Social Sciences. In addition to publishing widely on the early modern period, he writes fiction, plays, and poetry. He lives in New York City.

Katherine Davey was born in Cape Town, South Africa and moved to the UK twice, once temporarily as a teenager and then again to do a post-grad, which she abandoned to work in publishing. She has been writing since she was a child and belongs to the long-established and professionally wonderful writing group called (for reasons she has never understood) Free Lunch, based in Hackney. She lives in Walthamstow, London, and is currently revising a novel for which she is seeking representation.

Roberta Dewa has always written fiction, and in her twenties published three historical novels with Robert Hale. While studying for various degrees she wrote and published poetry and short fiction, including a poetry sequence on the explorer Shackleton and a short story collection, *Holding Stones* (Pewter Rose Press, 2009). In 2013 she published a memoir, *The Memory of Bridges,* and a contemporary novel followed: *The Esplanade* (Weathervane Press, 2014). Since retiring last year from teaching at the University of Nottingham, she has been writing poetry and short stories again, some of it inspired by (but attempting no comparison with) the sublime lyrics of Scott Walker.

Douglas Hill lives in the north-east of Scotland and worked in the regional press as a journalist and editor for many years. Before that he worked as a freelance reporter in Glasgow and wrote features for a number of magazines in the UK and abroad. Born in Scotland, he has also lived and worked in South Africa, Brazil, New Zealand, Spain, and for several years in London. Since devoting more time to writing fiction, he's been short-listed for a number of competitions, won 2nd place in the Exeter Writer's competition, and had short stories published in Writer's Forum.

Paul J. Martin moved to London from Northern California to earn an MA in Novel Writing from City University freeing himself from a high-flying career in the art world to pursue his passion for writing. Residing for many years in American suburbia he is fascinated to know why people live where they do. His work tends towards *Suburban Noir*, where he delves behind conformist facades and investigates strange tales and complications that lurk behind the mailbox. His first novel 'When I'm Calling You' is complete, his second follows close behind and he has a growing catalogue of short fiction from both sides of the Atlantic.

Gerard McKeown is an Irish writer living in London. His work has been featured in 3:AM, The Moth, and Litro, among others. In 2017 he was shortlisted for the Bridport Prize. He is currently seeking representation for his novel 'Licking The Bowl'. More of his work can be viewed at www.gerardmckeown.co.uk

Roland Miles has worked as an English and Drama teacher and as a dealer in secondhand books. He has an MA in Creative Writing from the University of Sussex. He is the author of *Chaucer the Actor: The Canterbury Tales as Performance Art*. Two completed young adult novels and a play sit unpublished in a box beneath his bed. A number of his short stories and flash fictions have been placed in competitions. He is currently close to finishing a collection of short stories about life in schools, of which *Trespass* is one. He lives by the castle in the Sussex town of Lewes, in a house built in the fifteenth century, once occupied by a bucket maker.

Meganrose Weddle has a BA in English Literature from the University of Cambridge and is studying for her MA in Creative Writing at Birkbeck, University of London. Her poetry has been published in creative journal *Notes* and she was shortlisted for the *Liars' League* Women & Girls event, for her short story 'No Strings Attached'. She lives and works in London and hopes, one day, that she can call herself a 'full-time writer'.

Lightning Source UK Ltd.
Milton Keynes UK
UKOW04f1111061217
313972UK00001B/4/P